"I wanted you last night."

"Don't say that!" she gasped.

"It's the truth! I've been wanting you more and more every day we've been together, but I can't overlook the fact that I forced you to accept this assignment. I've done my damnedest to control my feelings because I could imagine what you might think, but I wasn't having much success last night, and that made me angry."

"So you looked for an excuse to lash out at me."

"That's the part I've regretted most." Max was drawing her closer, tilting her face up to his, and her blue eyes widened in alarm when she felt his warm breath on her mouth. He saw that look, and released her. "What is it that you're afraid of, Kerry?" he asked quietly.

YVONNE WHITTAL, a born dreamer, started scribbling stories at an early age but admits she's glad she didn't have to make her living by writing then. "Otherwise," she says, "I would surely have starved!" After marriage and the birth of three daughters, she began submitting short stories to publishers. Now she derives great satisfaction from writing full-length books. The characters become part of Yvonne's life in the process, so much so that she almost hates coming to the end of each manuscript and having to say farewell to dear and trusted friends.

Books by Yvonne Whittal

HARLEQUIN PRESENTS

1022—SUNSET AT IZILWANE
1038—ELDORADO
1118—THERE IS NO TOMORROW
1149—TOO LONG A SACRIFICE
1358—SHADOW ACROSS THE MOON
1438—VALLEY OF THE DEVIL

HARLEQUIN ROMANCE

2441—THE LIGHT WITHIN
2478—THE SPOTTED PLUME
2538—HOUSE OF MIRRORS
2616—RIDE THE WIND
2742—WILD JASMINE
2922—BID FOR INDEPENDENCE

YVONNE WHITTAL

Far Horizons

Harlequin Books

TORONTO • NEW YORK • LONDON
AMSTERDAM • PARIS • SYDNEY • HAMBURG
STOCKHOLM • ATHENS • TOKYO • MILAN
MADRID • WARSAW • BUDAPEST • AUCKLAND

Harlequin Presents first edition October 1993
ISBN 0-373-11594-6

Original hardcover edition published in 1992
by Mills & Boon Limited

FAR HORIZONS

Printed in U.S.A.

CHAPTER ONE

KERRY NELSON felt irritable, and she cursed softly to herself as she drove along the M1 towards Johannesburg's illustrious suburb of Houghton.

As a freelance photographer she had many varied and interesting assignments, but on this particular Saturday afternoon she would have preferred to stay at home with a good book instead of having to venture out in the heat that prevailed in southern Africa at this time of the year.

She had wound down the window of her trusty old Peugeot station-wagon in an attempt to cool the interior of the vehicle, but the midsummer air was too hot. It wafted through the heavy strands of Kerry's fair, shoulder-length hair without easing her discomfort, and her generous mouth curved in a grimace at the clamminess of her body beneath the blue viscose of her short-sleeved dress.

She took the turn-off to Houghton, and found herself thinking dispassionately that this weather was ideal for the garden wedding Mrs Stafford had arranged.

Weddings were not Kerry's forte. There were many photographers who specialised in this field, she had argued when the widow of wealthy industrialist William Stafford had approached her some weeks ago, but Kathleen Stafford had been very persuasive.

'My daughter is absolutely adamant,' she had announced, the inflexion in her voice cleverly matching the plea in her grey-green eyes. 'Mary-Joe insists that she wants *you*, Miss Nelson, and no one else.'

Kerry had finally succumbed to that plea, but she was still doubting her decision when she eventually parked her blue station-wagon beside a high stone wall in one of Houghton's tree-lined streets.

She was taking her camera bag out of the back of the station-wagon when she heard Josie Bauer saying caustically, 'I was beginning to think you'd never get here.'

Kerry swept her hair away from her face and glanced at her wristwatch. 'I'm ten minutes *early*,' she protested with an amused chuckle while she locked the vehicle, but the smile on her lips faded when she turned to face her journalist friend.

Josie was wearing her red hair cut and styled in an attractive bob to frame her equally attractive features, but her face seemed unnaturally pale in the bright sunlight. Her smile was brittle, and her emerald-green eyes were also much too bright.

Kerry had known Josie Bauer for too many years not to recognise the signs. Josie was labouring under a tension which was aroused solely by the belief that she was on the verge of achieving the impossible in her career.

Kathleen Stafford had provided Kerry with a comprehensive list of the guests who would be attending the wedding, and Kerry sifted through it mentally while she held her friend's fevered glance, but she failed in her attempt to discover the reason for Josie's obvious tension.

'What's all the excitement about, Josie?' she demanded curiously, picking up her camera bag and settling the strap comfortably on to her shoulder. 'I'm sure you've lost count of the many society weddings you've had to attend in the past. What's so special about this one?'

Josie's brittle smile deepened as they walked towards the spiked wrought-iron gates which had been opened wide to welcome the wedding guests. 'Maxwell Harper's going to be at this wedding, that's what's so special about it, and I'm hoping I can persuade him to agree to an interview.'

'Maxwell Harper?' Kerry echoed the name softly, the memory bank in her mind whirling in recognition, but it failed in this instance to produce the required answer.

'Don't pretend you've never heard of the man.' Josie waved her hands agitatedly as she spoke. 'I happen to know you have quite a selection of his books in your private library at home.'

Kerry halted abruptly, the look of confusion in her eyes changing to one of incredulity as she faced her friend. 'Not M J Harper, the famed travel writer and producer of televised expeditions?'

Josie nodded and breathed excitedly, 'Yes, yes, yes!'

It took a moment for Kerry to recover from her surprise so that they could continue walking up the long gravel drive which took them past the blue and white striped marquee that had been erected on the freshly mown lawn of the enormous, sun-drenched garden.

Maxwell Jonathan Harper was a travel writer whose work Kerry had admired for a long time. He wrote knowledgeably and with an easy style, and his descriptive passages were so vivid that she had often had the sensation that she was seeing and experiencing everything for herself. She had been hooked after reading his first book, and her growing collection of his work now numbered among some of her prized possessions.

'What makes you so sure he'll be at the wedding?' Kerry wanted to know, her face and arms stinging in the heat of the sun as they approached the magnificent two-storeyed house with its pillared entrance.

'Maxwell Harper happens to be Mrs Stafford's brother. That makes him the bride's uncle and, since William Stafford is no longer alive to give his daughter away in marriage, it's only natural that Mary-Joe would ask her famous uncle to do the honours,' Josie explained.

Kerry took a couple of seconds to digest this new piece of information before she directed a mocking glance at her friend. 'I'm aware of how thorough you are when it comes to researching a subject before an assignment, so I believe it's safe to assume you have it on good authority that Maxwell Harper agreed to his niece's request?'

'He most certainly did agree.'

There was a hint of defiance in Josie's green eyes, and Kerry no longer suspected that she had been used—she knew it. 'So this is the reason you were so keen for me to obtain Kathleen Stafford's permission for you to do an article on her daughter's wedding! You wanted to make sure you'd be on hand to get a crack at interviewing Maxwell Harper.'

'Naturally.'

Kerry paused at the foot of the shallow marble steps that led up to the imposing entrance of the house, and could not disguise her deep displeasure when she directed her narrowed blue gaze at her friend. 'Why didn't you tell me this before?'

Josie's green glance did not waver. 'Would you have helped me to get this assignment if I had told you?'

'Most certainly not.'

'Need I say more?' asked Josie, a touch of familiar arrogance in her smile.

Kerry shook her head in helpless resignation. It would be pointless to remain angry with Josie. She was a good journalist with a reputation for achieving where others in her profession had failed, but in this instance Kerry was convinced that her friend was attempting the impossible.

'If I were you, Josie, I wouldn't raise my hopes too high about persuading Maxwell Harper to agree to an interview,' Kerry warned as they ascended the shallow steps to the entrance of the Stafford mansion. 'I know that some of our most noted journalists have followed him from location to location across the world, but I also know he's never granted any of them an interview.'

'I'm aware of all the facts,' sighed Josie, 'but I have to give it my best shot. Can you imagine the boost it would give my career if he should agree to talk to me?'

Yes, Kerry could well imagine what this would do for Josie's career. It was her sincere wish that her friend's enthusiasm and determination would be aptly rewarded, but she had read somewhere that Maxwell Harper was a man who guarded his privacy with a fierceness which made her doubt that Josie would succeed in this instance where more experienced journalists had failed.

Kerry rang the doorbell, and seconds later the heavy oak door was swinging open beneath the hand of a uniformed maid. They stated their business before they were invited into the cool interior, and Kerry could almost feel Josie's tension become her own as they were ushered through the tiled, spacious hall, past marble statuettes and up the curved, carpeted staircase where valuable landscape paintings and family portraits adorned the walls.

In a large, airy bedroom on the upper floor the bride was standing in front of a full-length mirror, while yet another maid was carefully fastening the tiny buttons up the back of an exquisite dress which, in Kerry's estimation, must have cost a fortune. The white beaded satin hugged the girl's figure, complementing her smoothly tanned shoulders, firm, full breasts and narrow waist.

Mary-Joe Stafford stepped away from the mirror to confront them when the last satiny button had been secured in its satin loop. She was an attractive, dark-haired young woman in her early twenties, and she smiled pleasantly when Kerry and Josie introduced themselves.

'You're gratifyingly punctual,' Mary-Joe remarked with a mischievous smile. 'My mother will appreciate the fact that you arrived on time, since she's convinced that she'll have become prematurely grey by the end of this day, with all the last-minute hitches she's had to endure since early this morning.'

They all laughed, and sharing this private little joke with the bride eased the tension in the room. It also left Kerry with steady hands for the photographs which had to be taken.

Mary-Joe Stafford was an easy subject to work on. She had a photogenic face, but her most charming feature was her pleasant and accommodating nature. Kerry was convinced that not many brides would have tolerated the disrupting presence of a photographer as well as a nosey journalist in their bedroom while they were preparing themselves for the most important day of their lives, but Mary-Joe seemed not to mind having to comply with their wishes while she added the finishing touches to her appearance. She looked calm and confident. She also looked radiantly happy and, just for an instant, Kerry envied her that happiness.

There were three bridesmaids in Mary-Joe's entourage, their figure-hugging satin dresses tastefully designed and ranging in colour from deep rose to pale pink. They filed into the bedroom while Mary-Joe's veil was being adjusted, and they brought with them an air of tempered excitement.

Kerry was actually beginning to enjoy herself while she positioned Mary-Joe and her bridesmaids for a series of photographs. It was only much later that she wondered about Josie, who had hovered studiously beyond the range of the camera's lens with her notebook and pencil and often probing queries. Had Josie enjoyed the task she had taken upon herself, or had she been impatient to begin her quest for that elusive interview?

The wedding guests had arrived, they had heard the cars crunching up the gravel drive towards the house, and Kerry was finishing off the roll of film in her camera when Kathleen Stafford entered the room. She was dressed in a pale green, lacy outfit which accentuated her remarkably youthful figure, and she acknowledged Kerry and Josie with a warm smile and a graceful inclination of her head before she turned her attention to Mary-Joe.

'I hope you're ready,' she said, the slight tremor in her hands belying the calmness of the attractive features which she had passed on to her daughter. 'Mr Abbot has just arrived and the guests are all seated.'

Kerry signalled to Josie, and they slipped out quietly to go downstairs. 'You go on ahead,' she suggested when they reached the hall.

Josie didn't quibble about that, and her eagerness to get away made Kerry smile as she carried her camera bag to a shadowy corner of the large entrance hall. She seated herself on a low, padded stool, working swiftly as she changed films and lenses on her cameras, and she was rising to her feet, her Leica dangling from about her neck, when she heard a door being opened on the upper floor. The sound of hushed but excited female voices drifted down into the hall, and she was smiling to herself while she adjusted the strap of her camera bag so that it would rest comfortably on her shoulder.

The front door opened before Kerry could leave and she turned to see a man in a dark grey suit entering the hall. She doubted she would have given him a second glance, but he halted abruptly in his long-legged stride to stare at her.

Her attention captured, Kerry stared back at him, her mind registering his wide shoulders and lean hips even while her glance settled on his features, and instant recognition made her heart leap wildly in her breast.

It was Maxwell Harper! Kerry would have known that tanned, ruggedly handsome face anywhere. His photograph was on the fly-leaf of one of his earlier books, and she had studied it often enough to believe she knew every angle of his lean face with the aquiline nose and square, determined jaw, but her conception of the lifeless image she had seen on paper was differing strongly from her conception of the man she was seeing in the flesh.

Maxwell Harper was only in his late thirties, but the brown hair cropped close to his head was already streaked amply with grey at the temples. Kerry realised that she was looking at the hard face of a man who had spent the greater part of his adult life witnessing bloodshed and destruction in various parts of the world, and she could see now that the horror, the futility, and the degradation of armed conflict had cut deep to leave a permanent scar.

The physical impact of his presence had a far more disturbing effect on her. That air of virile masculinity that surrounded him had a magnetic quality about it that drew her to him mentally, if not physically. Kerry tried to ignore it, but it tugged relentlessly at something inside her until, for the first time in her life, she felt her body responding in a way that sent an embarrassing warmth stealing into her cheeks.

Beneath the straight, dark brows his dark eyes had been alert, missing nothing, but it was not until his perfectly chiselled mouth quirked with a suggestion of a smile that Kerry was suddenly startled into the realisation that he had been observing her just as intently as she had been observing him.

How accurate his appraisal of her had been would remain something she could only guess at. The intimacy of her own embarrassing response was more than enough for her to cope with at that moment, and she could almost have cried out in relief when Kathleen Stafford caused a diversion by coming down the stairs ahead of the bride and her entourage.

Maxwell Harper turned his solid-looking back on Kerry to confront his sister as she descended the last few steps into the hall, and Kerry used this opportunity to escape, forcing herself to walk calmly out of the house even while the desire to run was so much stronger.

That encounter in the hall could not have lasted for more than a few seconds, but it had been long enough for Kerry to realise that Maxwell Harper was not a man she would wish to tangle with at any time in the future.

The two hundred guests had been seated beyond the marquee in a shady section of the garden where the ceremony would be conducted, and Kerry's pulses were still pounding a little wildly when she skirted the area to position herself in a strategic spot from where she could take photographs of the bride when she finally walked down the grassy aisle on her uncle's arm.

Where was Josie?

Kerry's glance hastily scanned the sea of faces, but she relinquished her search seconds later when a flutter of excitement among the guests made her realise that Kathleen Stafford had arrived to take her seat.

There was an expectant hush, and then Mary-Joe appeared under the makeshift arch on which the crimson roses appeared to be ranking so profusely.

The Reverend Mr Abbot rose from his chair and stepped on to the podium. He asked everyone to stand, and then the bride, with her ladies in attendance, walked slowly down the aisle to the recorded strains of the *Bridal March*. Kerry had her camera ready, but her hands started to shake when she encountered Maxwell Harper's imposing frame through the viewfinder.

Focus on the bride, Kerry! she told herself. Concentrate, and focus on the bride!

Mary-Joe's attractive features seemed to glow with happiness through the misty veil that covered her face as she approached the handsome young man she was about to marry, and Kerry's hands steadied, the professional side of her taking charge, but afterwards she was never quite sure how she had managed to accomplish her task with Maxwell Harper's dominant figure constantly in sight.

Kerry stood in the shade of an old jacaranda tree close to one of the several entrances to the marquee.

The wedding reception had been in progress for some considerable time. The guests were seated at decoratively laid tables, and they were in a jovial, almost rowdy mood while the refreshments were being served. Stewards were constantly on the move, offering champagne, and someone had solicitously placed a glass in Kerry's hand. She had not wanted it, but she sipped at it absently while her searching glance scanned the faces belonging to the cream of Johannesburg's society.

Where *was* Josie? Kerry controlled her agitation with difficulty. It was time to go, but she didn't want to leave without having a word with her friend.

'Miss Nelson?' Kerry turned and almost spilled the contents of her glass down the front of her dress when she saw Maxwell Harper standing a couple of paces away from her. She was too startled to respond immediately, and a quizzical look entered his eyes. 'You *are* Miss Kerry Nelson, aren't you?' he asked, lessening the distance between them.

'That's correct,' she said, holding her glass with both hands to steady it while she made a concerted effort to regain her composure.

'May I introduce myself? I'm——'

'I know,' she cut in, her nerves strung so tightly that there was a sharp edge to her usually warm voice. 'You're Maxwell Jonathan Harper, travel writer and one-time political correspondent for an overseas newspaper.'

It was his turn to look startled, and his heavy eyebrows lifted a fraction above eyes that continued to see too much. 'You're obviously well informed,' he commented.

At close range his masculinity was a great deal more potent. It set off a responsive flare inside her, and she had difficulty resisting the urge to turn and run.

'Your photograph and a brief biography was on the fly-leaf of one of your books,' she heard herself explaining the origin of her knowledge.

His eyes were a warm brown with flecks of gold around the pupils, and the creases beneath them deepened when he smiled.

'Did you read the book?' he asked, intruding on her observations with a trace of mockery in his voice. 'Or did your interest fade on the first few pages?'

'I read the entire book,' she said, keeping to herself the fact that she had not only read it, but that she possessed and had read all eight of the books he had written in almost as many years.

There was a tiny scar beneath his left eye and another along the right side of his strong jaw. It heightened the appeal of his rugged good looks, and Kerry had difficulty in maintaining an outward calmness while her pulses fluttered like a bird trapped in a cage.

'Perhaps you'll allow me to surprise you with *my* knowledge,' he continued in his deep, well-modulated voice. 'You're Kerry Ann Nelson, one-time photographer for a local fashion magazine before you started freelancing, and I must confess that your photographic exploits over the past two years have impressed me a great deal.'

Kerry wondered if she looked as startled as she felt. It was understandable that she should have a certain knowledge of him as a writer. He was, after all, quite famous. But how did he acquire his knowledge of her?

Her sense of humour fortunately came to her rescue and her facial muscles relaxed in a wry smile. 'You appear to be equally well informed,' she told him.

'I attended the first exhibition of your work two years ago. Your photograph was on the programme and I read the equally brief biography.' He had chosen his words to match her own, and Kerry might have laughed if she hadn't been so tense. 'I've been wanting to meet you ever since,' he added, 'but our paths never crossed long enough for me to arrange a meeting.'

She was instantly on her guard. 'Why would you have wanted to meet me?' she queried.

'It's quite simple.' He smiled as if he had sensed her wariness and knew the reason for it. 'I like the quality of your work sufficiently to want to engage your services as a photographer.'

Rejection flared inside her at the mere thought of working in close proximity with this man, and she shook her head. 'I don't think I could——'

'Hear me out, please.' He moved closer with some urgency, and Kerry, tall herself, was placed in that uncommon position where she had to tilt her head back to meet his glance. 'I'm writing a book on Namibia, but there's a certain amount of data I still have to collect, so I'll be leaving for Windhoek again shortly. It shouldn't take me longer than a month to complete my research, and I would want you to accompany me on this trip to take the necessary photographs.'

Kerry stalled for time while searching for a way to escape from this problem. 'What happened to the chap who dealt with the photographic side of your books in the past?' she asked.

'Dennis Cawley?' Maxwell Harper's mouth tightened derisively. 'He got himself married two years ago, and now his wife's had a baby he's had to curtail his travelling activities.'

The thought of marriage and having a family didn't appeal to this man—it was written all over his good-looking face—and Kerry felt a stab of disappointment. He was just like her father, who had turned his back on love and commitment while in pursuit of his career, and this was all the more reason why she did not want to become involved with a man like Maxwell Harper. He spelt trouble for her, she was thinking as she directed her gaze towards the marquee where the bridal couple circulated among their guests, and she had known enough pain and disappointment in her past to last her a lifetime.

'Would you consider accepting this assignment?' he pursued.

'I'm honoured that you should ask me, Mr Harper, but I'm afraid I can't,' she replied coolly, placing her champagne glass on the tray of a passing steward and walking towards the garden bench where she had left her camera bag.

She had to put some distance between Maxwell Harper and herself—she needed the space to think, but he followed her with an annoying determination.

'I'd like to know the reason for your rejection,' he said, obviously not accustomed to taking no for an answer.

'I'm fully booked for the next two months.'

'I'll double whatever you make in a month.'

Kerry spun round to face him, her blue eyes sparking with sudden anger. 'Money has never been a deciding factor,' she snapped.

'My publisher will also draw up a contract in which a certain percentage of the royalties will be assigned to you.' His dark, compelling glance held hers. 'All I'm asking is that you'll consider cancelling your other assignments to accompany me on this trip.'

'I'm sorry, but I can't do that.'

'Why can't you?'

Why was he being so persistent? There were plenty of photographers with impressive qualifications in Johannesburg. Why did it have to be her?

'I don't work that way,' she argued, her voice clipped with nervous tension. 'When I accept an assignment it's a commitment I make, and I don't just opt out of my commitments.'

'Oh, come now!' he mocked her. 'I'm offering you the opportunity of a lifetime and you're turning it down because of a few silly scruples?'

'That may be so, but the choice is mine!'

There was an awkward, angry silence between them which was broken only by the sound of voices and laughter emanating from the marquee, and it was Kerry who looked away first to avoid the probing query in Maxwell Harper's disturbingly dark eyes.

Josie emerged from the marquee at that moment, her glance darting about as if in search of someone, and Kerry seized this opportunity to escape. She picked up her camera bag and lifted the strap on to her shoulder, but when she turned she found Maxwell Harper observing her with narrowed, speculative eyes.

Kerry could imagine what he must be thinking. He probably considered her lacking in ambition and perhaps also a little mad to throw away such an adventurous—not to mention lucrative—opportunity, but at that moment she was too desperate to get away from him to care about how he might interpret her refusal.

'You'll have to excuse me,' she said, turning to leave.

'Just a moment.' Fingers of steel detained her. They snaked about her arm, biting gently but firmly into the soft flesh above her elbow, and a thousand little sparks of electrified energy seemed to be charging along the hitherto unexplored canals of her nervous system. He released her just as suddenly, cutting off that paralysing current to extract a card from the inside breast pocket of his immaculately tailored jacket. 'Give me a call when you change your mind,' he said.

Not *if* she changed her mind, but *when*! His arrogance left Kerry speechless as he turned on his heel and strode away to rejoin the celebrations. She stared down at the card he had thrust into her hand and felt like throwing it away, but instead she slipped it into the side-pocket of her camera bag before joining Josie in the cool shade of the marquee.

'I saw you chatting to Maxwell Harper, but you parted company before I could come along and ask for an introduction.' Josie's glance was curiously intent. 'May I hope you were putting in a good word for me?'

Kerry's nervous tension suddenly found its release in unaccustomed anger. 'I thought we'd agreed a long time ago that we would never meddle in each other's careers.'

Josie looked surprised, but then she smiled and linked her arm through Kerry's. 'You're quite right to put me in my place,' she said. 'I'll walk you to your car, and on the way you might satisfy my curiosity just a teeny bit by telling me what you and Maxwell Harper were discussing so earnestly.'

Kerry felt the tension uncoil inside her as they took a short cut across the lawn towards the wrought-iron gates. She was conscious of the fact that Josie was waiting with a rare show of patience for her to speak, but it was not until she deposited her camera bag in the back of the station-wagon that she managed to relate what had occurred between herself and the man whose work she had admired for so long.

'Maxwell Harper asked me if I'd consider accompanying him on a trip to Namibia to do the photographic side of his new book,' she said, wondering why her voice suddenly sounded like a frightened whisper.

Josie drew an audible, excited breath, and she was almost bristling with curiosity when Kerry slid into the driver's seat to insert the key in the ignition.

'And are you?' she demanded impatiently, her knuckles whitening where they rested on the door. 'For goodness' sake, don't keep me in suspense! Did you accept the assignment?'

'I turned it down.'

Josie's hands fell away from the door and her jaw dropped a fraction before she managed to pull herself together again. 'Are you *crazy* or something?' she demanded on a shriek.

'Perhaps,' Kerry responded tersely, winding down the window before she slammed the door shut.

Crazy? Irrational? Illogical? She could not decide which description suited her best. Her reasoning was not at its best at that moment, but there was one thing she was absolutely sure of: she would be in deep trouble if she took this assignment which Maxwell Harper had offered her.

She turned the key in the ignition, and the throbbing of the Peugeot's engine seemed to bring Josie back to life.

'May I call in at your place on my way home for a cup of coffee and a chat?' she asked, and Kerry's taut features relaxed in a smile.

'Consider yourself invited,' she agreed.

CHAPTER TWO

THE two-bedroomed cottage in the suburb of Bryanston had been in a dreadful state of disrepair when Kerry had seen it for the first time five years ago, but there had been something about it that had appealed to her, and she had bought it with the money from her mother's estate which had been held in trust for her until she was twenty-one.

The roof had needed extensive repairs, the plumbing had had to be renewed, and the entire cottage had needed to be rewired electrically. The cost of these repairs had depleted Kerry's inheritance, and the installation of the new security locks on the doors had left a dent in her savings which had been sizeable enough to call a halt to any further plans she might have had at that time.

It had taken all of four years, and every available cent Kerry had possessed, to complete the renovations. She had furnished the rooms in pale, restful pastels, using plain colours rather than florals to create the illusion of space where there was none. It had taken time, money and energy, but she had never regretted it. This was now her home. It was the base from which she worked. And she loved it.

The shrill, persistent whistle of the electric kettle brought her out of her reverie with a start. She had showered and changed into a cool cotton housecoat after her return from the Stafford home earlier that afternoon, but her hair was still tied up in a makeshift knot on her head and her feet were bare when she leapt up out of her comfortable armchair to dash into her small, compact kitchen.

She switched off the kettle and stared for a moment out of the kitchen window to where the sun was dipping low over the roof-tops of the houses. She had been expecting Josie to call in for a cup of coffee on her way home, but it was getting late, and she wondered...!

The chiming of the doorbell was a welcome intrusion on the thoughts siphoning through her wary mind, but the tension aroused by those thoughts seemed to linger on as she left the kitchen to admit her visitor. 'Don't panic—it's only Josie!' she scolded herself in an effort to calm her racing pulses, and a quick glance through the peep-hole confirmed this.

'I'm dying for a cup of coffee!' Josie exclaimed as she stepped into the small entrance hall with its cane telephone table beneath a blown-up photograph of three riders on horseback against the backdrop of the snow-capped Drakensberg mountains. 'Am I too late?'

'You're just in time.' Kerry closed the door and locked it securely before she led the way into her small kitchen.

Josie hooked the strap of her sling bag over the back of a kitchen chair and seated herself wearily, while Kerry spooned granules of instant coffee into mugs.

'I'm exhausted,' Josie complained when they finally sat facing each other across Kerry's small circular table. 'I should have gone straight home, but I thought you might be interested to learn that I managed to have a few words with Maxwell Harper.'

Kerry had wondered about this. 'Did you have any luck?' she asked with a forced casualness.

'Oh, he's courteous and charming, but he's a tough nut to crack when it comes to granting an interview.' Josie took another sip of coffee and stared fixedly at the bright yellow tablecloth. 'Maxwell Harper may believe he's seen the last of me, but I'm determined to try again.'

'Do you think it's wise to pursue him?'

'It may not be wise,' laughed Josie, looking up from her fixed contemplation of the tablecloth, 'but I'd be an absolute fool not to risk it.'

Kerry retreated mentally. This was not her territory, and she had no right to intrude. 'I imagine you know what you're doing,' she conceded quietly.

'I picked up a snippet of information which might interest you,' Josie announced into the silence that had settled between them. 'I had a moment alone with the bride before she left on her honeymoon, and in the excitement she let it slip that her uncle—meaning Maxwell Harper—had agreed to support her on her wedding-day on condition that she hired you to take the photographs. Now *that* suggests to *me* that he wanted to create an opportunity to meet you. What do you think?'

Kerry's insides were being strangled in the grip of a strange tension. Maxwell Harper was obviously a man who stopped at nothing to have his own way. 'I don't think it was nice of him to make such a stipulation,' she said at length.

'But it did give him the opportunity to meet you,' Josie persisted as she leaned back in her chair and eyed Kerry speculatively. 'As a matter of interest, why wouldn't you accept the assignment he offered you?'

The kitchen was becoming dismally dark, and Kerry got up quickly to switch on the light. She also gained herself a little more time to find a suitable excuse which would satisfy her friend's curiosity and halt her probing queries.

'The prospect of having to travel around Namibia for a month really doesn't appeal to me,' she said, avoiding eye contact with Josie when she sat down again at the table.

'What's suddenly happened to that adventurous spirit of yours, Kerry? Do you expect me to believe you've lost it?'

'I have commitments here in Johannesburg.'

'Oh, don't give me that feeble excuse!' Josie brushed aside Kerry's reply with a hint of scorn in her voice. 'I know for a fact that you've cancelled or postponed commitments many times in the past to traipse off into the wilds with your camera.'

Kerry could not refute that statement, and neither could she deny that she had been looking for an opportunity to explore Namibia. If the offer had been made by anyone else she would have jumped at the chance, but instead it had come from...!

'It's Maxwell Harper, isn't it, Kerry?' That was a statement, not a query, and Kerry looked up with a start, her expression unguarded in that instant when she met Josie's probing glance. 'So help me, it's true!' Josie exclaimed, sitting up with a jolt and staring at her with an incredulous look in her eyes. 'I believe there was something about that rugged, sexy hunk that must have got to you, and I think you're scared!'

'That's ridiculous!' Kerry's protest exploded from her lips in something close to alarm as she leapt up from her rigid perch on the edge of the chair.

'But it's true, isn't it?'

Kerry deposited her empty mug in the sink and stood with her back to Josie while she fought down that wave of heat which had surged into her cheeks. She knew the futility of lying, and she also despised it. Besides, she reasoned, Josie knew too much already.

'All right,' she confessed on an agitated sigh as she turned to confront her friend. 'There's something about the man that attracts me, and I admit I'm scared enough not to want the opportunity to explore it. Does that satisfy you?'

'You're no longer a child, Kerry, you're twenty-six, and you can't spend the rest of your life running away from every man who attracts you because of one serious relationship that went wrong.'

A look of distaste flashed across Kerry's sensitive features at the memory of Peter Forrester. 'I'm being cautious, that's all,' she shrugged.

'Being cautious is one thing, but shutting men out of your life is another,' Josie argued with her.

'I don't shut men out of my life.'

'Don't you?' Josie challenged Kerry mockingly. 'When was the last time you went out on a date with a man?'

'I... well, I——'

'You can't remember, can you?' Josie pounced on her triumphantly.

'OK, so I can't remember,' Kerry conceded defeat, 'but I'm scared of being hurt again.'

'Aren't we all?' Josie drawled conclusively, rising to her feet, but even in high-heeled shoes she stood half a head shorter than barefooted Kerry.

'Thanks for reminding me that I'm not unique,' Kerry responded coldly, but she was forced to recall that Josie had had her own fair share of heartache.

'You can be a pain at times,' Josie announced with a rueful smile as she lifted her bag off the back of the chair and slipped the strap on to her shoulder. 'You're also the best friend I've ever had,' she added, 'and I'd like to keep it that way.'

'I'd like to keep it that way too.' Kerry's rigid features relaxed into a smile as she linked her arm through Josie's and accompanied her to the door.

Their arguments were few, and then they never could stay cross with each other for very long. They knew each other too well and their friendship had spanned too many years for them not to make allowances for the irrevocable differences between them.

Josie's departure left Kerry in a disturbed frame of mind. She had something to eat and washed the dishes, but Josie had exposed an old scar, and now Kerry could not halt the memory of that unpleasant incident in her past.

She had been twenty-one at the time, and the fashion magazine she had worked for had staged a fashion show in which the winning model would receive a free trip to Europe as well as a good chance to further her modelling career at one of the famous fashion houses in Paris.

The travel agency allotted for this purpose had sent along a representative from one of their many branches in the city to deal with the flight arrangements, and that was how Kerry had met Peter Forrester, that charming, golden-haired Adonis whom all the girls had been so crazy about.

Their relationship had started with an invitation to lunch, and within a matter of weeks it had progressed to the stage where she had actually believed he would ask her to marry him.

Kerry had been so madly in love with Peter that she had ignored the visible signs that something was amiss in their relationship. There had been those evenings when Peter had cancelled their dinner arrangements, and the many weekends when their plans to spend time together had gone awry because he had had to go away on business.

This had gone on for months, until one fateful morning when Kerry happened to be working in the vicinity of Peter's office. He had insisted that she refrain from calling on him at his office, since his superiors disliked the idea of the travel agency staff receiving visits from family and friends during working hours, but on that particular morning, after four days of neither seeing nor hearing from him, she had felt driven to ignore his warning.

The first shock had been the discovery that Peter was in charge of the agency, and not someone else, as he had led her to believe. Trusting and gullible as Kerry had been, she had been prepared to overlook this lie, but the second shock had shifted everything into horrifying perspective for her.

On Peter's desk, and positioned in such a way that she could not fail to see it, had been a studio portrait of his wife and children.

He had tried to bluster his way out of it, but Kerry had seen him at last for the scoundrel he was. It had suited him not to honour his commitment to his wife and family, and neither would he commit himself to anyone else.

She had not seen him again, but it had taken months to recover from that experience and the knowledge of how close she had come to losing her self-respect.

A year later she had heard by chance that Peter had taken a transfer to Cape Town and this his wife had had another child. So much for his talk of divorce! Kerry had thought cynically, and after that the healing process had quickened its pace, but she had never fully regained her trust in men.

And now there was Maxwell Harper.

No! She did not want to think about him!

She sought refuge from her thoughts by closeting herself in her darkroom, but she was checking the prints she had pegged up to dry earlier that day when she realised that there was no point in trying to hide from the truth.

The fact that she had been well acquainted with Maxwell Harper's photograph on the fly-leaf of one of his books had not prepared her for the shock of meeting the man in person, and neither had she been prepared for the physical response his presence had awakened in her.

Kerry leaned back against the cupboard and closed her eyes briefly. The intensity of her feelings had frightened her, and it still frightened her merely to think of it.

She was not naïve enough to imagine that she could spend four weeks alone with a man like Maxwell Harper without something happening between them. The attraction had been too strong to ignore; the magnetism too powerful to resist. Her inexperience would count against her, and that would make her an easy conquest.

An easy conquest? Kerry was startled by her own thoughts. Was that what she would be? The answer that flashed through her mind strengthened her decision not to accept the assignment. She had considered her armour impenetrable, but Maxwell Harper had proved her wrong.

Kerry did not sleep very well that night, and it rained so much on the Sunday morning that she had to cancel her trip into the country. She spent the day at home instead, but found she could not relax, and every time the telephone rang she was afraid she might hear Maxwell Harper's voice on the line.

She was being ridiculous. Why would he call? She had given him her answer, it was final, and he must know that nothing he could say would make her change her mind. She had no cause to feel uneasy, or even guilty, she remonstrated with herself. She was a free agent, and no one could force her to accept an assignment which she did not want. Not even Maxwell Harper.

She went into the kitchen to make herself a cup of coffee, but there was no escape from the disturbing thoughts that plagued her.

Damn! Why couldn't she get Maxwell Harper out of her mind?

Kerry's workload the following day left her with no time to think about anything else, and she was simply too tired to care about the weekend's nagging uneasiness when she finally emerged from her darkroom shortly after four that Monday afternoon.

She wandered into the kitchen to switch on the kettle. All she wanted at that moment was to take the weight off her feet, and a few minutes later she sat curled up comfortably in her favourite armchair, sipping coffee and listening to the recorded messages on her answering machine.

The first call was an invitation from an old college acquaintance to attend a reunion dinner, and the second was in the form of an SOS from Calvin MacCullum, co-editor of the fashion magazine where Kerry had once worked.

'A bumbling idiot has landed us in the most calamitous situation, darling,' he said, his Scottish accent more pronounced in his anger. 'We're in desperate need of a fashion photographer at the Carlton Centre tomorrow morning. I shan't leave the office until I've heard from you, and I pray to God you can help us.'

Kerry was smiling when Calvin's message ended, but her smile faded when she heard the excited delivery of the third message on the tape.

'Hello, Kerry—Josie here. I've a luncheon date with Maxwell Harper, and I can scarcely believe my luck! I'll call you later to tell you all about it.'

Kerry's uneasiness returned with a vengeance. It knifed through her sharply and left in its wake a feeling that came close to fear. It seemed so unlikely that Maxwell Harper would capitulate without a struggle after years of stoically refusing to have the private side of his life reviewed by the public.

Kerry's palms felt clammy with nervous perspiration, and she tightened her grip on her coffee-mug. Did she have reason to be uneasy about this meeting between Josie and Maxwell Harper? Or was she simply underestimating Josie's powers of persuasion?

She shelved her thoughts hastily and made an attempt to concentrate on the remaining contents of the tape in the answering machine, but minutes later Josie's second recorded message shot the problem back into the forefront of her mind.

'Kerry, it's Josie again. I've got to see you this evening—it's urgent. I'll be there at seven. Bye!'

Kerry moved without being consciously aware of it. She lowered her feet to the carpeted floor, and she was sitting on the very edge of her chair when Josie's message came to an end. Josie had stressed the urgency to meet with her that evening, but Kerry had detected something more than mere urgency in her friend's voice. Anxiety?

Stress? Kerry could not be sure, but she was beginning to have a nasty suspicion that it involved her personally.

'Stop it! You're becoming neurotic!' she rebuked herself angrily as she put down her mug and got up out of her chair. There were more important things to do than sit about creating imaginary problems, she decided as she wiped her clammy palms on the skirt of her pink zip-up coverall and marched into the small entrance hall.

She flicked through her diary on the telephone table. Her appointments for the following morning could be postponed to accommodate Calvin MacCullum's urgent request and, lifting the telephone receiver, she punched out his number to collect the details for the assignment.

There had been several other messages that required her response, and Kerry dealt with them all before going into the kitchen.

She normally enjoyed cooking for herself, but on this particular evening she was far too edgy to bother. She prepared a quick salad and placed a dish of left-over stew in the oven before taking a shower and changing into something else.

The white cotton frock with the blue and green floral sash tied about the waist had been designed for casual wear, but on Kerry's tall, slender body it looked chic enough for a garden party. The gentle curve of her hips made the calf-length skirt flare elegantly about her long, shapely legs, while the V-necked bodice had been styled to allow for the thrust of her small, firm breasts.

She brushed her hair to a silvery sheen and applied a light touch of make-up before slipping her feet into white low-heeled sandals, and she was smiling to herself when she walked out of her pale pink and ivory-white bedroom to sit down to her solitary meal in the kitchen. She had no idea what the evening had in store for her, but she was not going to let it get her down.

It was a brave thought, but all too soon she lost her grip on it.

Kerry had watched the six o'clock news on her portable TV while she ate her dinner, and she had left the set switched on as a form of distraction while she washed the dishes and wiped down the cupboards. On reflection she realised that she had had more than two hours to rid herself of those nagging fears for which she could find no substance, but her calmness was no more than a veneer when Josie arrived shortly after seven that evening.

There was a plastic security card clipped to the wide collar of Josie's brown silk blouse. That meant that she had come directly from work. Her face looked grey in Kerry's dimly lit entrance hall, and her shoulders sagged as if she was carrying a load which was too heavy for her small, feminine frame.

'You look exhausted,' Kerry commented as she led the way into the lounge where she had dimmed the lights earlier to create a relaxed atmosphere.

'I could do with a drink.' The words spilled from Josie's lips on a groan as she collapsed on to the sofa and stretched her legs out in front of her. 'Do you have any of that brandy left over from the last Christmas party we had here?'

'I think I saw a bottle somewhere.' Kerry's curiosity was more than just a little aroused, but she held back all those burning queries while she walked around the sofa to get to the old oak dresser she had inherited from her mother. She opened one of the doors and went down on to her knees to peer inside. 'Yes, here it is,' she said, reaching into the far corner of the cupboard and producing the half-forgotten bottle of brandy.

'I'd appreciate it if you'd pour me a drink, but make it a stiff one with ice and no more than a dash of water,' Josie told her.

Kerry's arched eyebrows shot up in surprise. This was an unusual request from someone who rarely consumed anything stronger than wine, but Josie's haggard expression endorsed Kerry's belief that the questions could wait until later.

She went into the kitchen to pour Josie's drink, and her mind broke free of the tight rein she had kept on it since that afternoon. Maxwell Harper was involved in this. She knew it as surely as she knew that the sun would rise again in the morning. The nature of his involvement still remained a mystery to her, but she had a feeling that she would know the answer soon enough.

She felt the tension spiralling inside her, and was not surprised to see her hand shake when she handed Josie her drink. She seated herself on the padded arm of the sofa and watched in silence while Josie gulped down a mouthful of the barely diluted brandy. Josie shuddered and pulled a face, but she poured a second mouthful of the amber-coloured liquid down her throat before she slumped back into the cushions of the sofa with an angry scowl on her face.

'What's wrong, Josie?' There was a nervous edge to Kerry's quiet voice, and Josie looked up briefly only to scowl down into her glass again.

'I've got a problem.'

Kerry's patience was wearing thin. 'I've already gathered that, so why don't you tell me what it is?'

'That's part of the problem,' Josie sighed, the ice tinkling against the sides of the glass as she twirled her drink in her hand. 'I don't know *how* to tell you.'

'Just spit it out, Josie, the way you always do.'

Josie swallowed down the remainder of her drink, but by this time her insides must have been sufficiently insulated not to evoke a shudder.

'Maxwell Harper's been doing some surface digging into our lives,' she said. 'He seems to think he can use the basis of our friendship as leverage to get what he wants, because he said he'd grant me an interview if I could persuade you to accept the assignment he offered you.'

Kerry understood at last, and she leapt to her feet as resentment exploded inside her. 'That's unfair!' she cried out, pacing the floor in her fury. 'That's *damned* unfair!'

'I doubt that he cares very much whether his method of persuasion is fair or foul. Maxwell Harper wants you for this assignment, and he's determined to get you.' Josie frowned down into her empty glass and pushed herself up on to her feet. 'I'll help myself to another drink, if you don't mind.'

How *dared* he? Kerry halted her senseless pacing and stood with her hands clenched at her sides as despair began to mingle with her fury. She was beginning to feel panicky, and it blinded her temporarily to the fact that Josie had left the room to return a few seconds later with her brandy glass replenished.

Josie sipped at her fresh drink while she kicked off her shoes and sank down on to the sofa. She was taking another substantial sip of brandy when she looked up for the first time that evening to meet Kerry's steady blue gaze.

'I told him I couldn't do it, Kerry,' she said quietly, answering the unspoken query in Kerry's eyes. 'I told him he could grant me an interview on my own merit, or not at all.'

'How did he react to that?'

'He said something about merit and good fortune being united, and that he had imagined I would have been clever enough to have recognised that fact long ago.' Josie gestured abruptly with the hand that held the glass and almost succeeded in spilling some of the liquid on to her beige skirt. 'I know very well what he meant, of course. He was simply using a more subtle form of persuasion by reminding me that I can't get by on merit in my profession if I ignore the opportunities that come my way.' She took a mouthful of brandy and swallowed it down, while her eyes sparked an angry green fire. 'Let's send him to *hell*, Kerry!'

Kerry would have liked nothing better at that moment, but Maxwell Harper's hard-bitten features were beginning to materialise in her mind, and the scars of conflict and suffering were there once again for the discerning and sympathetic eye to see.

'I think he's been to hell and back already,' she murmured softly, unintentionally giving voice to her thoughts.

'What?' Josie blinked her eyes as if she was having difficulty trying to focus on Kerry. 'What did you say?'

'It was nothing.' Kerry waved aside her query and quelled the sudden desire to laugh hysterically. 'It was just a silly observation.'

Josie's silent acceptance alerted her to something she had been too preoccupied to recognise before. Josie was not accustomed to drinking strong alcohol, and she had been imbibing rather heavily for someone who had probably had nothing to eat since lunch that day.

'What are we going to do about Maxwell Harper?' Josie asked, a faint slur in her voice as she raised the glass to her lips with an unsteady hand, and Kerry kicked herself mentally for allowing this to happen to her friend.

'If you drink any more of that brandy you won't be in a fit state to drive yourself home,' she warned, seating herself again on the padded arm of the sofa.

'It doesn't matter,' Josie announced with a strange little laugh as she started to slide sideways on to the cushions. 'I think I'll just pass out here on your sofa anyway.'

'Oh, no, you won't!' Kerry rescued the glass from Josie's fingers before the brandy could spill out on to the sofa. 'You're coming with me into the kitchen,' she said, taking her friend firmly by the hand and dragging her up on to her feet. 'You need to pour some strong black coffee down your gullet instead of brandy, and you're going to eat something. You're welcome to spend the night on my sofa if you're not sober enough to drive yourself home, but I'm damned if I'm going to let you pass out on me before we've had a chance to talk this thing out.'

'What's there to talk about?' Josie's query was argumentative, but she offered no resistance when Kerry half dragged, half carried her through the small entrance hall and down the short passage into the kitchen. 'Maxwell Harper can go to the devil for all I care! I don't *want* this stinking interview!'

'Oh, yes, you do!' Kerry contradicted sharply as she pulled out a chair and pushed Josie into it. '*I* know how much you want that interview, *you* darn well know it, and so does Maxwell Harper! He's got us in a cleft stick,

Josie, and right now I guess he's sitting back and enjoying the thought of how we must be wriggling.'

'He's putting a strain on our friendship to achieve his own goal.'

'Exactly.' Kerry's fine-boned features wore a grim expression as she poured the contents of the brandy glass down the sink and switched on the electric kettle. 'I have the distinct feeling that we're being put to the test, and that's going to be the main point of discussion. Now I suggest you shut up and don't say another word until you've got something besides alcohol in your stomach.'

Josie seemed only too willing at that moment to let Kerry take charge, and Kerry plied her with mugs of strong black coffee while she warmed what was left of the stew. She prepared a fresh salad, and having something to do relieved part of her tension and anger, but the reality had to be faced in the end.

'I'm not hungry,' Josie had complained, but half an hour later she had polished off the meal Kerry had prepared for her. She was forcing down her third mug of coffee when her eyes met Kerry's across the table. 'I'm sorry,' she said, smiling apologetically. 'If you hadn't stopped me I'd have got myself totally drunk, and that would have been a dumb thing to do.'

'You'll probably wake up tomorrow morning with a headache to prove exactly how dumb it would have been.'

'Thanks for that comforting thought.' Josie's smile was almost a grimace, and when it faded her face wore a sombre expression. There was a brief, awkward silence between them, then she steered the conversation back towards the problem which was foremost in their minds. 'I don't want you to accept an assignment that you don't want, Kerry.'

'And I don't want you to lose this opportunity to interview Maxwell Harper,' Kerry countered quietly, but not without a certain amount of inner anxiety.

'Our friendship is strong enough for me to survive the disappointment,' Josie assured her.

'Is it?' Kerry felt driven to question that statement as she crossed her arms in front of her on the table and leaned towards Josie. 'Is *any* friendship strong enough to survive this kind of disappointment?'

'*Ours* is,' Josie insisted, her emerald-green glance unwavering over the rim of her coffee-mug.

Kerry could have left it at that. Everything inside her was crying out for her not to pursue the matter, but her conscience would not allow it.

'That's how you feel now, Josie,' she persisted, even though she dreaded where it would lead. 'How will you feel if, at some future date, a fellow journalist should have the honour of being the first to interview Maxwell Harper? How will you feel knowing that, but for me, that honour could have been yours?'

Josie's thoughtful gaze shifted to a point beyond Kerry's shoulder before she looked away completely and lowered her mug to the table with a thud that almost spilled some of the coffee on to the yellow tablecloth. 'I think I'm in need of another strong drink,' she groaned.

'No, you're not!' Kerry's hand shot out to grip Josie's wrist before she could push back her chair and get up. 'We've always been honest with each other, Josie. That's why our friendship has survived all these years. Please—for both our sakes—be honest with me now.'

'The truth?'

Kerry nodded in reply, and the tension-packed silence seemed to go on for an eternity before Josie raised her glance from the tablecloth with a look of desperation in her eyes.

'I think I'd hate you if someone else walked away with the honour,' she said with the honesty Kerry had demanded of her.

'Thank you, Josie,' Kerry sighed as she released her grip on Josie's wrist and leaned back in her chair.

Josie stared at her with a look of incredulity on her face while she absently massaged her wrist where Kerry's fingernails had dug into her flesh. 'You can sit there and thank me after what I've just said to you?' she queried.

'I'd have said the same if our roles had been reversed,' Kerry replied with the same blunt honesty she had demanded of Josie. 'That, I believe, is the true meaning of friendship.'

Her mind was like an octopus reaching out with its tentacles in a tentative exploration. It touched on danger and withdrew instantly, but it reached out again, knowing that the danger had to be confronted.

She surfaced from that brief, contemplative silence to realise that she had somehow given Josie an insight into her thoughts. Her friend's face registered a mixture of intense relief and growing excitement, but the flush receded just as swiftly from her cheeks to leave her pale with self-loathing.

'Oh, God, *no*!' Josie buried her face briefly in her hands and tried to compose herself, but her cheeks were still ashen when she looked up at Kerry. 'You're going to take that assignment so that I can get my *damned* interview!'

'You'd have done the same for me,' Kerry pointed out.

'I doubt it!' Josie contradicted sharply, self-derision thinning her lovely mouth. 'It's that selfish streak inside me that made me come here this evening. I should have stuck to my decision and left it at that—but no! I *had* to involve you because subconsciously, I think, I *wanted* you to help me out, and right now that's the part of me I hate most!'

Kerry shelved her own anxieties to concentrate on Josie with genuine compassion and understanding. 'Don't hate yourself for being human, Josie. We all set goals ourselves, and right now I happen to be standing between you and your goal. It doesn't matter if the desire to make me change my mind was subconscious or deliberate. What matters is that you shouldn't feel bad about it.'

'I don't deserve a friend like you, Kerry.' Josie's eyes filled with tears and she rose quickly to her feet. 'I think I'd better go home. I feel like bawling my eyes out, but I'm sure you've had enough drama for one night.'

Kerry stood in her dimly lit entrance hall. She was tapping the small card between her fingers against the thumbnail of her other hand, and she was staring at the small digital clock beside the telephone. Ten-fifteen. Was it too late in the evening to make a call? Well... too bad!

She lifted the receiver and her eyes were as cold as the snow-capped mountains in the blown-up photograph against the wall as she punched out the number printed on the card.

The telephone rang a few times before it was answered. 'Maxwell Harper,' that now familiar voice announced.

'Kerry Nelson,' she responded with equal abruptness.

'This is an unexpected pleasure.'

Liar! she felt like shouting at him. You've been waiting for this call because you knew it had to come!

'We have to talk,' she said instead with an icy hostility in her voice. 'When can we meet?'

'Tomorrow,' he said. 'My place or yours?'

'Neither,' she answered him coldly, but her insides had responded with a treacherous warmth to that undertone of sensuality she had detected in his voice. 'There's a coffee bar at the Carlton Centre. It's called Rico's. Do you know where it is?'

'I'll find it.'

'Meet me there at twelve-thirty.'

'I'll be there,' he said.

Kerry dropped the receiver back on to its cradle. It was done! She was no longer just touching danger, she was grasping it with both hands, and after tomorrow there would be no turning back.

CHAPTER THREE

KERRY ran to catch the lift in the Carlton Centre, her finger jabbing at the control button to halt the doors before they could slide shut. Faces registered annoyance at having to accommodate one more passenger in a lift which was already filled to capacity, but Kerry ignored this as she squeezed herself into the nearest corner between the control panel and an oversized woman with a double layer of pearls underlining her double chin.

The lift started its smooth, swift descent, and that hollow feeling at the pit of Kerry's stomach seemed to shoot up into her mouth to make her swallow convulsively.

A sleepless night had left her raw around the edges, and she was amazed that she had survived the photographic session that morning with all its frustrating delays. Her nerves had been stretched to their limit, and it didn't help to know that she was fifteen minutes late for her appointment with Maxwell Harper.

Twelve floors down the lift slowed to a seemingly abrupt stop, and Kerry's sensitive insides settled back into their normal position with a sickening lurch that left her a little dizzy when she stepped out the lift and made her way toward Rico's.

Her heart was thudding uncomfortably hard against her ribs. Being late for this appointment would place her at a disadvantage, and that was not what she had envisaged when she had planned this meeting with Maxwell Harper. He was not going to be an easy man to deal with, and she had needed every advantage she could get. It was a pity she had failed in this instance, but there was no point in letting it upset her, Kerry decided when she entered the crowded coffee bar with its panelled walls, soft, low-hanging lights and tempting aroma of freshly ground coffee beans.

Maxwell Harper was seated at a side-table beneath a large poster of a matador caping a bull, and Kerry saw him the instant she walked in. He was dressed casually in a blue lightweight jacket and white open-necked shirt, but he had lost none of that dangerous appeal she had encountered at their first meeting.

Kerry took a firm hold on herself. She was prepared for this confrontation, she was in control, but she could not prevent that odd fluttering deep down inside her when he looked up and saw her making her way towards him among the tables.

He rose from his chair, his dark eyes meeting hers briefly before she felt their heat trailing her body. Her pulses fluttered in response to that visual touch, and she was suddenly intensely aware of the fact that a sleepless night and a frustrating morning had not left her looking at her best.

She had not asked him to meet her here to impress him with her appearance, Kerry had to remind herself sharply, but she could not help wishing that her white cotton trousers and green striped shirt could have retained some of their crispness during the course of the morning.

'I apologise for making you wait so long, Mr Harper.' Her voice was cool and clipped with the effort to control those helpless tremors which his mere presence could arouse in her.

'So it wasn't intentional?'

The gleam of mockery in his eyes did not escape Kerry as they sat facing each other across the small table, and her first reaction was anger, but then the charitable side of her nature had to acknowledge that she might have given him cause to imagine that her late arrival had been deliberate.

'I was unavoidably delayed,' she felt compelled to explain, and his oddly probing glance held hers a moment longer before he broke the contact to raise a summoning hand for the waitress.

'Would you like something to eat with your coffee?' he asked when the waitress had threaded her way through the crowded coffee bar to their table.

Kerry shook her head. 'Just coffee, thank you.'

He ordered two cups of coffee, and waited until the waitress had left before he captured Kerry's glance once again. 'I suggest we skip the pleasantries and get right down to the reason you asked me to meet you here today.'

'I agree,' she said, disliking the feeling that Maxwell Harper seemed to be taking command of a situation which she had wanted to control.

'I believe you know the contents of the conversation I had with Miss Bauer?' he prompted, his glance resting on her hair which she had tied back casually at the nape of her neck with a white scarf.

'Yes, I know.' She wondered if her hair had come undone when she saw his dark brows draw together in a slight frown, but she resisted the temptation to check. 'You made a deal with Josie. If she could pressurise me into doing the photographic side of your book on Namibia, then you would grant her an interview. Quite frankly, Mr Harper, I think your method of persuasion is despicable.'

'I thought again that it was rather clever.'

That unperturbed, faintly mocking rejoinder aroused her to anger and disappointment. Did he not feel the slightest twinge of remorse?

'Moral blackmail isn't clever, it's simply disgusting.' Her voice was icy with disapproval. 'Do you always stoop this low in your attempts to get what you want?'

'Only when there's been an absolute need for it. Your friend is pestering me for an interview while I'm in need of your photographic expertise, so we made a deal.'

He smiled suddenly, and it defused her anger to send a bone-melting warmth surging through her body. She tried to look away, but she couldn't. She was noticing how his smile softened the harsh angles of his rugged features and deepened the little creases at the corners of his eyes. Did he have to be so damned good-looking?

The waitress brought their coffee to their table and left, but that brief diversion afforded Kerry the much needed opportunity to regain her control. She helped herself to milk and a little sugar, but Maxwell Harper drank his coffee black and unsweetened. Was that a habit which had been forced on him during the years he had been a political correspondent?

She had to stop this, she warned herself angrily. She had to stop noticing and questioning so many things about him. If she had any hope of saving the situation for Josie and herself then she dared not lose her sense of direction.

'What made you think Josie might have the ability to make me change my mind?' she asked, purely to satisfy her curiosity.

'I know your friendship goes back to the days when you were at school together.' The look of surprise that flitted across Kerry's face brought a gleam of mockery to his eyes. 'I have a reputation for being good at ferreting out certain information,' he added.

'That's obvious,' she murmured, recovering swiftly, 'but that doesn't exactly answer my question.'

'I know how a journalist thinks, and my determination to guard my privacy has unfortunately made of me a prime target for those who seek recognition for themselves. From where I'm standing at the moment it all seems quite ridiculous, but the challenge has been circulated, and your friend wouldn't have been worth her salt as a journalist if she'd ignored it.' He was leaning towards Kerry and his eyes were probing hers with an intensity that made her suspect he was attempting to strip away the barriers that guarded her soul. 'Can you deny her this journalistic feather in her cap and continue with your friendship as before?'

He had touched on a very sensitive issue, and Kerry felt the jolt of it reverberating along her tautly strung nerves. 'I was hoping I could reason with you, and that you'd consider granting Josie the interview if I recommended a good photographer who——'

'Forget it!' His deep voice was low and harsh as he shredded her only hope. 'The deal includes you, or there's no deal at all!'

'You're not being fair!' she protested, but it did nothing to soften the relentless set of his jaw.

'If I can agree to having my much desired privacy invaded, then I can't imagine why you should find it so difficult to cancel or postpone your other engagements in favour of the assignment I'm offering you.'

Kerry fell silent. There was a certain fairness in that statement which she could not dispute, but it did not ease that feeling of helplessness inside her. She was like a fly caught up in a spider's web, and it seemed that no amount of wriggling was going to set her free.

Kerry was aware of the people around them. She could hear snatches of their conversation and the occasional burst of subdued laughter. Everything seemed so normal and relaxed as opposed to the inner turmoil she was experiencing at that moment while they sat drinking their coffee.

There was an antagonistic tension in the air between Maxwell Harper and herself. There was also that undeniable spark of physical awareness between them, and it was threatening to rob her of the ability to think rationally, especially when she felt his eyes resting on her, willing her to look at him.

He pushed his empty cup aside, and Kerry stared for a moment at that strong, sun-browned hand resting on the table. He had long fingers that tapered down to square nails which he kept clean and clipped short. She could remember the firm, detaining grip of those fingers on her arm. Their touch had been electrifying, almost painful, but she had no doubt that they could also be gentle. How would it feel to have those fingers exploring her body? Stroking her skin?

She collected herself hastily, but not before the intimate trend of her thoughts had sent a rush of embarrassing warmth surging into her cheeks. Nothing like this had ever happened to her before, and she could only pray that the lights in the coffee bar were dim enough to conceal her shame.

'Do you accept the assignment, or don't you?'

Kerry raised her head sharply and her embarrassed glance collided with his. She had been wedged firmly into a corner, but she was still searching desperately for a means of escape. 'Do I have to give you an answer now?' she asked.

'There's a flight out to Namibia next week on Monday, and I want to be on it.'

His heavy-lidded eyes gave the impression that he hovered somewhere between boredom and laziness, but Kerry was not fooled by that look. His dark eyes had lost none of their alertness, and he was quick to notice the nervous tremor in the fingers she curled about her coffee-cup. He knew the next move was hers, and he seemed content to wait, reminding her in this instance of a predatory animal waiting with infinite patience for its prey to make that inevitable move which would deliver it into capture.

A bubble of hysteria rose sharply inside her, seeking an outlet, but Kerry swallowed convulsively to force it down. She was trapped, and there was no point in trying to deny it.

'I don't have a choice,' she said, staring hard at the checked tablecloth as she took that final and inevitable step towards her own capture. 'I'll accept the assignment, but I'll want a guarantee from you that you'll honour your part of the agreement with Josie Bauer.'

'Look at me, Kerry.' It was the unexpected use of her first name rather than the harsh command in Maxwell Harper's deep voice that startled her into doing as she was told. 'You have my word on it. Josie Bauer will get that interview before I leave for Namibia.'

Kerry searched his dark eyes, but she found nothing there to contradict his statement. Her fate was sealed, and she would simply have to resign herself to the inevitable.

'You have a deal, Mr Harper,' she said at length, 'but I think I deserve to know the reason why you refused to settle for anyone else.'

An odd expression flitted across his ruggedly handsome features, and the silence was threatening to become awkward between them when he suddenly leaned forward across the table to peer into her cup. 'Have you finished your coffee?' he asked.

There was a mouthful of the aromatic brew left in her cup, but she felt certain it would choke her if she drank now. 'Yes, I'm finished. Why do you ask?'

'Come with me,' he said, rising to his feet, and there was something so commanding in his manner that she felt compelled to obey him.

Kerry waited while he paid the bill. She might have looked outwardly calm, but nervous tension was eating away at her insides when she accompanied him out of the coffee bar. Where did he want to take her? And why?

Questions pounded through her wary mind, but they dried on her lips as he gripped her arm just above the elbow and ushered her out of the building at a pace that forced her into a run at times to keep up with him.

'Where are we going?' she demanded, breathless and curious and very much aware of those strong, lean fingers which seemed to be branding her flesh when they reached the car park.

'You wanted to know the reason why I wouldn't settle for anyone else, and I have something to show you which I believe will give you the answer you're seeking.' He released her arm as he spoke and transferred the disturbing warmth of his hand to the small of her back while he guided her towards a silver-grey Mercedes.

'I have to be back here at two for a photo session,' she hedged, fighting down the panic inside her.

He raised his left hand and the sun glinted for an instant on the slim gold watch strapped to his lean, sun-browned wrist. 'I'll have you back long before then,' he told her.

The Mercedes had a comfortable, roomy interior, but Kerry felt robbed of sufficient space to breathe normally when Maxwell Harper got in beside her and closed his door.

She leaned back in her seat as they drove away from the Carlton Centre. She was making a conscious effort to relax, but she could not ignore that powerful aura of masculinity which emanated from the silent, stern-faced man beside her, and neither could she ignore her own response to it.

She tried to concentrate on the route they were taking, but instead she found herself making an unobtrusive study of Maxwell Harper. She would have liked to believe that her observation was casual, but she had to face the disquieting truth and admit to herself that she was registering every detail about him with more than simply her mind.

He had taken off his jacket, and his white short-sleeved shirt seemed to cling too tightly to his wide shoulders and muscled biceps. Dark hair curled against his tanned, sinewy forearms, and those strong, long-fingered hands had taken control of the steering-wheel with a sure, easy touch.

Sure and easy. Those hands would take control of a woman in exactly the same way until she was stripped of any desire to resist.

Kerry felt an odd tightness gripping her chest, but she could not alter the direction of her thoughts. Was there someone special in Maxwell Harper's life? Did he have a woman waiting at home to welcome him back from those numerous and lengthy trips all over the world?

It was none of her business, she told herself, but she couldn't help wondering, and it was with some difficulty that she dragged her glance away from those long, muscled thighs straining against the confining cloth of his grey trousers.

She stared out of the window beside her and was confused by her surroundings until she managed to recognise a few landmarks. They were in the vicinity of Ellis Park and heading towards the centre of the city. Where was he taking her? What was it he wanted to show her?

A few minutes later Maxwell Harper was parking his car at the entrance to a yellow bricked building. It was an expensive-looking block of flats. People lived here. Kerry turned to the man beside her, expecting an explanation, but he collected his jacket off the back seat and got out of the car without saying a word.

She had no choice except to follow suit, but she was shivering despite the warmth of the sun against her body during those seconds before they entered the building and walked towards the lifts. Her mind was running riot when one of the lift doors slid open in response to Maxwell Harper's finger on the button, and a gnawing suspicion was beginning to take shape in her mind when she realised that she was being whisked up to the twenty-second floor.

The silence between them had become protracted and tense, and it seemed to take an eternity rather than seconds before the steel cage ceased its upward motion beneath her feet. The lift doors slid back, and Kerry almost leapt out of her skin when she felt Maxwell

Harper's hand touching her arm to guide her out into the carpeted foyer.

She was vaguely aware of the fact that there were three flats on that floor, but there was nothing vague about the hand on her arm which was propelling her towards the panelled door facing the lift. Her quickened heart-beats restricted her breathing, but she could no longer restrain the need to know the answer to that nagging query at the back of her mind.

'Are you taking me to meet someone, or do you live here in this building?' she asked, not daring to look at Maxwell Harper for fear that he might glimpse the nervous apprehension in her eyes.

'I live here when I happen to be in Johannesburg.'

Panic caught at her throat, stifling any response she might have made as she watched him unlock the panelled door and give it a push so that it opened wide.

'After you,' he said with a trace of mockery in his glance.

Kerry hesitated, but her hesitation lasted for no more than a fraction of a second before she preceded him into the flat. She was determined not to let him see that he had unnerved her, but she flinched visibly when she heard the soft click of the door being closed behind them.

If she had expected to see a feminine touch in Maxwell Harper's luxury flat, then she would have been disappointed. He had chosen serviceable leather and solid wood to furnish the spacious lounge, and the colours ranged from deep tan to a pale cream. It was a totally masculine domain, but Kerry liked it. It was a room she felt she could have relaxed in if it were not for her host's disturbing presence.

She could not recall afterwards whether it had been by accident or design that she found herself standing beside a low cabinet of Oriental origin. Above the cabinet, mounted against the wall, was a blocked enlargement of a black and white photograph. Kerry's glance skipped over it idly, then shot back with interest, and she drew a startled, hissing breath as she recognised her own work. The enlargement had been one of the many photographs she had exhibited for the first time two years ago, and she could recall vividly how difficult it had been for her to part with it.

'So it was you!' Her incredulous statement was directed at Maxwell Harper, while she continued to stare at the photograph with that mixture of surprise and pleasure which one usually encountered at a chance meeting with an old friend. '*You* bought it!'

The subject was an old man seated on a park bench with one heavily veined hand resting idly on a cane while he watched a group of young children clambering over a nearby jungle gym. The eyes were thoughtful in the wrinkled face, almost sad, but the mouth quirked in a smile as if he remembered his own youth and found something there to amuse him.

Kerry knew the scene so well. She had lived with it from that memorable afternoon when she had captured it on film in the park and on through all the stages of development. She had studied the finished product so many times while it had still been in her possession that every detail, and every emotion it had aroused would remain with her forever.

'I detected an accusation in your voice.' Maxwell Harper stood directly behind her and her nostrils quivered with the pleasing scent of his masculine cologne when he asked, 'Do you dislike the thought that I was the one who purchased the photograph?'

'If I sounded accusing, then it was unintentional,' she said apologetically, incapable of taking her eyes off that wrinkled face against the wall. 'None of the photographs on exhibit had been for sale, and this one also happened to be a particular favourite of mine.'

'I gathered as much from the price I paid for it.'

The amusement in his voice did not escape her, and guilt and embarrassment stained her cheeks a deep pink as she recalled her frantic reaction two years ago when the gallery owner had approached her with the news that he had a buyer for the photograph.

'The outrageous price tag was intended to act as a deterrent,' she explained when she recovered her composure.

'It made me all the more determined to have it, and it's worth every cent I paid for it.'

Kerry turned and glanced up at him with a certain amount of surprise. He wasn't joking, he was serious, and something about the way he was looking at her made her ask, 'Is this what you wanted to show me?'

'Yes.' He held her glance while he gestured with his hand towards the photograph. 'Doesn't this explain why I wouldn't settle for anyone but you?'

'That depends on what you might be looking for,' she responded cautiously, not wanting to commit herself until she understood his form of reasoning.

'I look for sympathy, compassion and understanding in the work a photographer produces, but what I look for most is sensitivity.' He gestured once again to the photograph mounted against the wall. 'This one says it all.'

Kerry was stunned by the compliment, and also a little intrigued. Maxwell Harper had not concerned himself with the technical side of her work; he had looked at it from a human angle, and he had uncovered sentiments which she had not been aware of before.

'No photographer would dare to guarantee all those facets in everything they produced,' she argued, disturbingly aware of that lean, muscular body within touching distance of her own.

'I'm not disputing that fact,' he assured her smoothly. 'To produce those qualities not only depends on the subject and the circumstances, but also on how much of yourself you're prepared to put into your work, and the latter naturally varies according to mood and temperament. I did, however, mention that what I looked for most was sensitivity, and that was something which I found in every one of your photographs.'

He was much too clever for comfort. He had given her the explanation she had asked for, and he had also used every trick in the book to give it the substance it required. He had coated it with honeyed words of praise, but he had added a large measure of logic which Kerry could not ignore. The nature of his books required more than the ordinary chocolate-box photographs, and Kerry would have had to be mentally stunted not to recognise the fact that she had the ability to give him what he wanted.

She turned away and tried to shrug off his remarks with a faintly cynical, 'I suppose I ought to feel flattered.'

'No!' He was behind her again in an instant, his fingers biting into her shoulders as he spun her round to face him. 'What I've told you is the truth as I see it. I've dealt in cold, harsh facts for too many years to want to settle for the falseness of flattery.'

Kerry looked into those hard, uncompromising features and realised her mistake. Facts were based on truth, and this man would not give any less than he received.

She suspected that he not only worked but lived by that rule, and she had thoughtlessly insulted him with her careless choice of words.

'I think it's time to go,' she said, breaking the strained silence between them. 'You said you'd have me back at the Carlton before two o'clock, and it must be nearly that.'

He released her at once, giving her room to breathe normally again while he glanced at his watch. 'We have twenty minutes, so I'll get you there with time to spare.'

They were silent again in the car during the drive back to the Carlton, but on this occasion Kerry was less aware of the man beside her and more concerned with the problem of her immediate future. She had given him her answer—for Josie's sake she had accepted the assignment, but she had a feeling she would live to regret it.

Maxwell Harper drove up to the entrance of the Carlton, and Kerry was getting out of the silver-grey Mercedes when he said, 'I'll be in touch as soon as I've made the necessary travel arrangements.'

She nodded without speaking, and as she walked away from him she prayed that she looked calmer than she felt.

Kerry had risked the heavy Saturday morning traffic in the city to make a few last-minute purchases, and she spent the rest of the weekend trying to select only the most essential items of clothing.

'Limit yourself to one suitcase,' Maxwell Harper had warned on the telephone. 'Remember that the terrain will often be rough and the heat could become unbearable, so I suggest you select sensible rather than fashionable clothes for this trip.'

Kerry was accustomed to travelling light. Once, while on a scenic hiking tour, she had had to live for almost two weeks out of a rucksack to accommodate her weighty camera equipment. Packing had not been a problem on that occasion, so it should not have posed a problem now; but it did.

She was in a rare state of nervous tension when Josie arrived unexpectedly on the Sunday evening with a Chinese take-away meal and a bottle of white wine.

'I hope you're hungry,' Josie said when she breezed past Kerry into the house, and Kerry was suddenly forced to recall that she had had very little to eat since breakfast that morning.

'I'm starving,' she confessed with a grin.

'Oh, good!' Josie glanced at the neatly folded shirt and trousers which Kerry held draped over her arm. 'I suggest you get on with your packing while I dump this lot in the kitchen and open the wine.'

Kerry's mood was much lighter when she returned to her bedroom to pack the last few items of clothing. She was glad that Josie had come. They had spoken briefly on the phone, but they had not seen each other since that night, almost a week ago, when Josie had been in a rare state of panic about Maxwell Harper's proposition.

Josie entered Kerry's bedroom some minutes later, and stared incredulously at the medium-sized suitcase that lay open on the bed. 'Is this all you're taking?' she queried.

'It's a good thing I'm not fussy about what I wear.' Kerry's smile was slightly twisted as she flipped down the lid of her suitcase. 'I've packed two non-crease dresses which ought to be suitable for the evening, but everything else is casual and guaranteed drip-dry.'

'I've always admired your ability to survive on the bare necessities.' There was a hint of envy in Josie's voice. 'Are you ready to eat?'

'Yes, please.'

They both had a lot to talk about, but they stoically avoided the subject of Kerry's departure until much later when they retired to the lounge with the wine which was left in their glasses. Josie curled herself up in an armchair, while Kerry settled herself on the sofa among her impressive array of camera equipment. Their conversation suddenly dried up and there was a long, uneasy silence before Josie asked, 'What time does your flight leave in the morning?'

'A quarter to seven.'

'Do you need a lift out to the airport?'

'I'm taking a taxi.' Kerry looked up from the lens she was cleaning and saw the look of frowning disappointment on Josie's face. 'It's all been arranged,' she added with a reassuring smile. 'The taxi will be here in good time to collect me.'

'I just wish there was something I could do. I feel as guilty as hell, you know, and I——'

'Don't!' Kerry interrupted her gently but firmly. 'You know I've always wanted the chance to go on a working tour through Namibia, and now I have it.'

'I know you've been hoping for this opportunity, but then you never planned on having Maxwell Harper as a travelling companion.'

'I'll survive.' Kerry brushed the matter aside with a careless lift of her slim shoulders. 'Let's talk about you instead. Did the interview with Maxwell Harper live up to your expectations?'

'Yes and no. He's extremely cagey about his personal life, so I still don't know very much about the man himself, but he's given me more than enough material to put together an extremely interesting article.' Josie sipped at her wine and flashed a smile at Kerry over the rim of her glass. 'I'm not complaining.'

'It's still an achievement.'

'Oh, I agree.' Josie's smile faded to leave her expression thoughtful. 'He's actually a very nice man, Kerry. He's easy to talk to and as straight as a die.'

Kerry thought it best not to respond to that remark, but agitation made her apply an unnecessary vigour to the task of cleaning her camera lenses while Josie persisted with her annoying observations.

'The two of you have so many similar interests that I couldn't help thinking you'd make an ideal couple. Don't you think you might——?'

'No, I don't!' Kerry interrupted sharply, dropping the lens and cleaning equipment into her lap and picking up her glass to take a steadying sip of wine. 'I'm content to stay the way I am until I meet the right man, and I shan't settle for anything less than a lifetime commitment.'

'How do you know Maxwell Harper isn't the right man? He's thirty-eight, he's single, and——'

'And he's likely to remain single for the rest of his life,' Kerry chipped in scathingly.

'What makes you think that?' Josie looked startled.

'It was something he said at his niece's wedding.'

That wasn't the complete truth, Kerry was thinking as she drank the last of her wine, but she had no desire now to elaborate on the subject.

'You could be wrong, you know,' argued Josie, but Kerry shook her head adamantly.

'I don't think so. He's committed to his work, and nothing else.'

'You've always been so rational and logical in your approach to everything in life that I find it rather odd to see you reacting this strongly about something which is a mere supposition.'

'I don't happen to be very rational and logical where Maxwell Harper is concerned,' Kerry was confessing before she could stop herself.

'If you're trying to fight off the attraction by making yourself believe the worst of him, then he must really have you rattled.'

Josie had a way of stripping things down to expose the often misshapen root of a problem, and Kerry was visibly shocked by what she saw.

'I don't know why I've allowed him to affect me in this way. God knows, Josie, I've tried to be rational about the whole thing,' she said, feeling compelled to explain her strange behaviour. 'I've been trying to convince myself that it was my admiration of his work that made me come close to acting like a swooning teenager the first time I saw him, but that explanation just isn't plausible. What I felt that first time wasn't the swooning adoration of a fan, and what I've felt since then has absolutely no connection with any form of hero-worshipping.'

'I think that sexy hunk has succeeded in awakening you to the fact that you're a normal woman with the correct amount of physical urges. Now, if it were me——' Josie struck a seductive pose and fluttered her eyelashes '—I'd go for the whole experience and enjoy it while it lasts.'

Kerry could not help laughing at that, but her laughter ended on an exasperated sigh. 'I'm not looking for an affair, Josie. This is purely a business relationship.'

'I notice you're not denying that you feel attracted to the man.'

'No, I'm not going to deny it, but I don't want to become emotionally involved with a man who'll take whatever he can get out of a relationship without giving anything in return.'

'Are you afraid you might fall in love with him?'

'I have nightmares about it,' Kerry admitted.

'God knows I could kick myself for being such a blind, self-centred idiot!' Josie leapt to her feet in anger to pace the floor, but she had gone no more than a few paces from her chair when she retraced her steps with an anxious look on her face. 'How are you going to handle the attraction when you're alone with him out there in the wilderness?'

'Badly, I think, and that's what really frightens me.' Kerry's expression was grave, then a nervous smile plucked at the corners of her generous mouth. 'On the other hand, I'm not going to lose sight of the possibility that I might be drumming up a storm with no clouds on the horizon.'

Josie stared hard at her for several seconds before she collapsed on to her chair with a groan on her lips. 'I think *I'm* going to be having nightmares until I know you're back safe and sound.'

CHAPTER FOUR

THE changing landscape far below the silver-winged Boeing had failed to capture Kerry's attention, neither could she do justice to the meal which the cabin crew had served to them. She was trapped between Maxwell Harper's imposing frame on her right and the window on her left through which the early morning rays of the sun slanted against the back-rest of the seat in front of her.

She had felt trapped from the moment they had boarded the plane at Jan Smuts airport less than an hour ago, when Maxwell Harper had edged her into the window seat. The pleasing hint of his masculine cologne had tantalised her senses, fanning her latent desire for escape, but his lean body had taken on the shape of a solid barrier, preventing her from changing her mind and making a last-minute attempt to fly the coop.

Kerry had belted herself into her seat and had sat rigid and silent during the first half of their flight to Windhoek. She had tried looking out of the window and she had tried to read, but nothing had registered with her except the sight of that hard, denim-clad thigh so close to her own and the electrified flaring of her nerves every time a muscled arm had brushed against her.

'You hardly touched your breakfast,' Maxwell Harper remarked when the flight stewardess had removed their trays.

'I wasn't very hungry,' lied Kerry, folding away the table and brushing an imaginary crumb from her beige trousers as she took her magazine out of the seat pocket in front of her.

'Would you like another cup of coffee?' he persisted, leaning towards her as he spoke, and she stiffened instinctively when she felt the hard warmth of his shoulder pressing against her own.

'No, thank you, Mr Harper.'

'Max,' he corrected her smoothly. 'My friends call me Max.'

Kerry's fingers tightened involuntarily on the glossy pages of the magazine she had opened on her lap. She had never had difficulty before in getting on to first-name terms with people, but with this man it seemed to suggest an intimacy which she did not want.

'You've hired my services as a photographer, and that places me in the category of an employee, not a friend,' she said coolly, turning a page of the magazine and using the action to ease herself a fraction away from that disturbing shoulder without making it obvious.

'Even my enemies call me Max.'

Enemies? Her first instinct was to laugh it off, but the possibility that he could have enemies was not quite so improbable when she paused to take his years as a political correspondent into consideration.

Kerry failed in her attempt to imagine his past life and she looked at him for the first time, searching his rugged features for the truth. 'Do you have many enemies?' she asked with unashamed curiosity.

'A few,' he smiled, his stern mouth relaxing and his eyes crinkling at the corners.

He has a nice smile, she was thinking. When he smiled at her like that it made her feel curiously warm inside, and it began to melt away that icy reserve she had been clinging to so desperately. There was no real harm in using his first name, was there?

Kerry lowered her gaze hastily to the pages of the magazine she was clutching in her hands, but her eyes were not focusing on the words printed there when she said with a forced casualness, 'If friend and foe alike call you Max, then I guess I'll have to do the same.'

'Say it again,' he ordered.

'Say what again?'

'My name,' he commanded, looking into her puzzled blue eyes. 'Say my name again.'

'Max,' she obliged him, even though she was startled by the request and more than a little confused.

'You make it sound like music!' he sighed theatrically, and wry humour replaced the puzzled look in Kerry's eyes when he feigned a swoon and sagged back into his seat.

'Does flying in a plane always affect you in this way?' she asked drily, the corners of her mouth quivering with the effort not to laugh.

'Only when I happen to be sitting next to a beautiful woman,' he replied, lifting his head off the back-rest to look at her, and his dark, warm glance lingered for a moment on her soft, quivering mouth before it dipped lower to where the glossy silk of her lilac blouse could not conceal the gentle curve of her breasts.

'This is a silly conversation,' she said, her voice clipped with the determination to control her fluttering pulses.

'You're right, this is a silly conversation, but that doesn't alter the fact that you're a beautiful woman.'

Kerry was beginning to feel awkward and uncomfortable beneath the direct appraisal of his dark eyes. 'Why don't you read a magazine, or—or something?' she muttered.

'If I've embarrassed you, then I apologise, but you're more relaxed now than you were fifteen minutes ago.' He leaned towards her again, his shoulder brushing against hers and his head lowered to observe her closely. 'Aren't you, Kerry?'

She paused to consider his statement and was surprised to discover that he had spoken the truth. 'Yes, I am more relaxed,' she admitted.

'What were you so tense about?'

'Several things,' she confessed.

'Such as?'

Kerry's inherent honesty would not allow her to lie to him, but she carefully selected the least important item on her list of grievances.

'I haven't forgiven you for blackmailing me into this assignment,' she told him.

'In that case we're quits,' he countered grimly, 'because I haven't forgiven you for forcing me into granting your friend an interview.'

'That isn't true! I never forced you into anything!' she protested hotly, glancing at him with indignation and anger mingling in her eyes.

'If you'd accepted the assignment in the first place, then I wouldn't have had to resort to such drastic measures to get you to agree.'

Kerry ought to have conceded defeat, but there was still too much fight left in her to even begin to consider it. 'There has to be a healthy balance in most things, so I imagine a loss is often followed by a gain, or vice versa.'

'That's an interesting philosophy, but let's look at it from *your* side,' he countered with a twisted, faintly mocking smile, and Kerry had a sinking feeling that he was going to win this argument when he started counting her benefits on his fingers. 'You're gaining financially for your photographic services on an all-expenses-paid tour of Namibia which will eventually lead to the public exposure of your work. What have you lost in the process to allow for that healthy balance you mentioned?'

'I'm not sure yet,' she said evasively, looking away and wondering how she would answer that question after spending every day of the next three weeks in his company.

'I suggest we forgive each other and call a truce on that subject,' he said, intruding on her frightened thoughts, and a strong, long-fingered hand appeared in her line of vision. 'A truce?'

'A truce,' she agreed after a momentary hesitation, placing her hand in his and liking the warm, rough texture of his palm against hers.

'I've noticed before that you have nice hands,' he said, gripping her wrist unexpectedly with his left hand and spreading her fingers across the palm of his right hand. 'They may be small, but they look strong and capable.'

'I'd like my hand back, please.' There was a calmness in Kerry's voice that belied the nervous quickening of her pulses when he turned her hand palm upwards.

'In a moment,' he said, tracing the path of that thin white scar across the width of her soft palm with the tip of one long finger. His touch was light, and it was arousing a sensation so pleasurable that it made her tremble inwardly. 'What caused this?' he asked.

'I ripped my hand open on a barbed wire fence.'

Her voice had emerged huskily from her taut throat, and her breathing had become oddly restricted while she stared in almost hypnotic fascination at that finger which was tracing that old, half-forgotten scar back and forth across her palm. It was like a slow, deliberate caress, and suddenly every receptive nerve in her body was centred on that spot in delightful anticipation.

Was he aware of his actions and of the devastating effect it was having on her emotions?

'What the devil were you doing on a barbed wire fence?' he demanded, a frown creasing his broad forehead.

'I had an enraged bull ploughing up the dirt at my heels, and I was too far from the gate to make a quick exit.' She tugged sharply at his restraining grip, impatient to be freed. 'May I have my hand back now?'

He released her, and she was beginning to breathe easier when he asked, 'How old were you when this happened?'

'I was fourteen.' The memory of that once frightening escapade washed over her, and a look of wry amusement flashed across her sensitive features. 'I'm adventurous by nature, but at that age I was also stupid.'

'Aren't we all a little stupid at that age?' His smile softened the determined, faintly ruthless line of his upper lip, but it also added a disturbing hint of sensuality to the curve of his lower lip. 'Tell me when and how your interest in photography began.'

Kerry lowered her gaze hastily from that sensuously chiselled mouth only to find herself staring at the dark body hair curling softly against his deeply tanned skin at the collar opening of his blue shirt. What would it feel like to run her fingers through it and to know the warm texture of his skin against her palm?

Stop it, *Kerry*! Don't do this to yourself! He's asked you a question and he's waiting for your response! Concentrate on that instead! she told herself.

She leaned back in her seat and stared out at the blue sky beyond the window while she forced herself to relax and recall the past.

'My mother bought me my first camera as a birthday present when I was ten.' Kerry's rigid features eased into a smile as she remembered the occasion. 'It was one of those auto-focusing cameras with a built-in flash, and at first I took photographs of anything and everything I saw, but in time I became more selective in my choice of subjects. When I was thirteen I was lucky enough to win a photographic competition, and the prize was a Nikon thirty-five mm single reflex lens camera that introduced me to a whole new dimension of photography.' She paused a moment for consideration before she added, 'I think that was the moment when I knew for certain that I wanted to make photography my profession.'

'Your mother must be very proud of you and of what you've achieved in your career,' Max said.

Kerry turned her head against the back-rest to look into those dark eyes which had been observing her so intently, but she looked away again when she felt the aching tightness of tears at the back of her throat. It was perhaps silly, but after all these years it could still hurt.

'My mother died during my first year at college,' she said, her voice brittle with the control she exercised. 'My inheritance was held in trust until I came of age. The monthly allowance I received barely paid for my studies, so I had to supplement my income by taking on assignments in my spare time.'

'Couldn't your father have helped?' he asked.

Kerry stiffened inwardly as she raised the barriers against a different kind of hurt. 'My father ran out on us when I was five, and my mother never married again.'

'Did you never hear from him again over the years?'

'I heard that he'd gone to Australia, and five years ago I succeeded in locating him with the help of a friend, but the feedback discouraged any attempt at making contact.' She absently fingered the magazine which lay forgotten in her lap. 'He's the managing director of his own structural engineering company, and I imagine he must be quite wealthy if he can afford to live in one of Sydney's élite suburbs. He's also married again with two teenage children, and the appearance of a daughter from his previous marriage would merely complicate his life.'

'Did he actually say that, or is this merely your own interpretation of his response?' asked Max.

'If my source of information was correct, and I have every reason to believe that it was, then I'm quoting him almost verbatim,' she said, hiding her pain behind a tight smile.

'I'm sorry.'

'He also said that since we hadn't seen each other for so many years we would be confronting each other as strangers, with nothing in common except the fact that I carried his name from a marriage he would rather forget.'

It had been curiosity and a vague yearning which had instigated Kerry's search for her father three years after her mother's death. There had been no photographs of him in their home, and her memories of him had been reduced to that of a shadowy figure with no substance.

'It was never my intention to intrude on his life, or to ask to become a part of it,' she said.

It was also none of Maxwell Harper's business what had prompted her to contact her father five years ago, but for some obscure reason Kerry could not curb the words that flowed from her lips.

'All I really hoped for was a brief meeting, to talk with him and to satisfy some crazy desire to know what my father looked like, but I suppose I was expecting too much.'

What's the matter with you, Kerry? she asked herself. You've just told this man something you've never even mentioned to Josie, and she's supposed to be your best friend!

'Did your mother ever tell you why your father walked out on their marriage?' Max questioned her, the deep velvet of his voice intruding on her angry thoughts.

'My mother told me it was an unfortunate clash of personalities, but she wouldn't say more than that, and I didn't want to pursue the matter when it was obvious to me that she still found it too painful to discuss.' Kerry's hands sliced the air in a brief unconscious gesture that indicated her desire to bring this particular conversation to an end. 'How the devil did we manage to digress from my interest in photography to the subject of my runaway father?' she added.

'One thing usually leads to another,' he said, looking into her stormy eyes and smiling at her with a warmth that was stripping away her anger to reveal an astonishing desire to weep.

The flight stewardess created a welcome diversion when she chose that moment to wheel a trolley down the aisle between the seats. Plastic cups and glasses rattled in the process of being stashed away in the trolley and, with Max's attention conveniently elsewhere, Kerry had an opportunity to regain control of herself.

She waited until the stewardess had moved further down the aisle before she glanced again at the strong profile of the man beside her. In a short space of time she had told him more about herself than she had revealed to others in her entire life. Why? What was it about him that had made her open up and spill it all out? And what did she really know about *him*?

'Are your parents still alive, Max?' she asked.

'No.' His sensually chiselled mouth tightened on that monosyllabic reply, and he did not follow it up with an explanation.

'Am I touching on a sensitive subject,' she probed curiously, 'or am I being subjected to a display of your normal reluctance to talk about yourself?'

He looked at her then, the dark eyes warning her to back off, and Kerry knew in some uncanny way what had prompted this reaction.

'I don't delve into someone's personal life on Josie's behalf. We may lean on each other in friendship, but we never make use of each other professionally.'

Her quietly spoken assurance made his eyebrows lift a fraction in surprise. 'How could you possibly know what I was thinking?' he demanded.

'Your thought-waves were coming across so loud and clear that I couldn't miss it,' she told him.

'I owe you an apology.'

'No,' she said, shaking her head. 'Your reaction was understandable.'

'Perhaps we could start this conversation again,' he suggested, and the smile that started in his eyes was soon easing the tautness about his mouth. 'You asked if my parents were still alive.'

'And you said they weren't,' she reminded him when he lapsed into a thoughtful silence. 'You don't have to talk about it if you don't want to.'

'It's not a subject I often dwell on, but there's nothing dark and devious about it.' His glance focused on her for a moment before he looked away. 'My father died in a helicopter crash when my sister and I were small children, and my mother died of natural causes a few years ago.'

There was more to it than that. Kerry had sensed the undercurrent of feeling which had accompanied that statement, and she felt driven to pursue the subject. 'What was your father doing in a helicopter?'

'He'd gone out on an assignment.' Max turned his head to look at her, but his expression had become shuttered, making it clear that there were certain things which he still considered too personal to divulge. 'My father was a political correspondent.'

Kerry controlled her features with difficulty, but she could not prevent that odd tightening in her chest. 'How did your mother react when she discovered you were planning to follow in your father's footsteps? Didn't she object?'

'She tried to talk me out of it by warning me that it was a lonely, often dangerous job, but there was nothing she could really do to stop me.' Max smiled twistedly. 'My mother had always known that I'd inherited my father's lust for excitement and far-away places, and she also knew that the craving inside me would never be cured if I made no attempt to satisfy it.'

'But you haven't satisfied that craving entirely, have you?' said Kerry.

'You're very astute.' His smile deepened and his bottom lip curved sensuously as he held her glance. 'No,

I haven't satisfied that craving entirely, and I doubt that I ever shall.'

The pilot's voice came over the intercom system in the Boeing to announce that they would be starting the descent towards Windhoek, and Kerry could not help wondering if there was something symbolical about that statement.

Was she perhaps starting her own precarious descent towards something which was as yet unknown; something which might very well change the course of her life?

The city of Windhoek lay surrounded by arid country, sheltered from excessive dry winds between the Auas and Eros mountains, but Kerry still found the air uncomfortably hot and dry as she stood at the window of her hotel room and watched the sun sinking slowly over this historical city on her first day in Namibia.

The Windhoek airport was situated at Ondekaremba, forty-four kilometres east of the capital, and they had landed punctually at twenty minutes to nine that morning.

Maxwell Harper had hired a taxi to drive them the distance from the airport to their hotel in the city, and after they had settled in he had left Kerry to spend the rest of the day as she pleased while he went to collect the Range Rover he had hired and purchased the necessary supplies for the trip. He also had to meet with a few officials to acquire certain necessary permits before their departure in the morning.

'If you have time you might care to study this,' he had said, thrusting a folded sheet of paper into her hands before he had left her at the hotel. 'It's a map of

Namibia, and you'll notice that I've marked the route we'll be taking.'

Kerry had had no objection to having the day to herself to explore the city at her own leisure. She had gone window-shopping and sightseeing during the remainder of the morning, and after lunch she had taken a stroll down the Kaiserstrasse with her Leica to capture on film the fascinating contrast in architecture.

There were buildings dating back to the first decade of the twentieth century with their steep roofs, small gables and dormer windows, and next to them had risen modern, multi-storeyed edifices. It was a pleasant mixture of old and new, the historical architecture of the German colonial past blending with the concrete and steel of the present, and to Kerry it felt as if they had spanned the decades with dignity.

The shadows lengthened into dusk, and an involuntary sigh escaped her when she turned away from the window. She was having dinner with Max at eight in the hotel's à la carte restaurant, and when she glanced at her wristwatch she realised that she had only a few minutes left to do something about her hair.

Her low-heeled silver sandals made no sound on the carpeted floor as she crossed the room swiftly to seat herself at the dressing-table. She switched on the small neon light above the mirror and checked her make-up before brushing her hair vigorously. She was going to tie her hair back again with a scarf, but she changed her mind and left it hanging free for a change.

She fingered the silky folds of her blue dress as she rose in front of the dressing-table, wondering if the V-neck was not too low when she caught a glimpse of that shadowy hollow between her breasts. She was beginning to feel both nervous and excited, and it was useless trying to tell herself that Maxwell Harper had nothing to do with it.

It was all quite ridiculous, she tried to reason with herself. The man was a comparative stranger to her, and yet she could not stop that fluttery feeling of anticipation at the mere thought of being with him again.

The summoning knock on her bedroom door made her start nervously and, snatching up her small silver evening bag, she hurried across the room with the flaring skirt of her dress wafting about her shapely calves.

Her heart was beating a little wildly in her breast when she opened the door to find herself looking up into Max's clean-shaven, ruggedly handsome features. His hair had been brushed back severely from his broad, intelligent forehead, while his beige lightweight suit and open-necked shirt seemed to accentuate the tanned fitness of his muscular physique.

Kerry was forced to recall her reaction the first time she had seen him in the hall of his sister's home. She was encountering that same sensual awareness now while they stood appraising each other, and that dark, calculating glance shifting over her body was arousing the same embarrassingly feminine response. Her skin was tingling as if he had touched her with his hands, and that curious ache in the lower regions of her body sent a weakness surging through her that made her long for something she dared not even begin to analyse.

'Shall we go?' he asked, gesturing with his hand and moving aside for her to emerge from her room.

Kerry nodded, not trusting her voice until she had managed to control her wayward emotions, and she prayed silently that her trembling legs would not fail her when she stepped into the carpeted corridor and closed the door behind her.

The sensuous, faintly mocking smile that softened the contours of his chiselled mouth had not escaped her. She suspected that he was fully aware of the effect he was having on her, and he was enjoying it. *Damn* him!

The restaurant seemed to be filled to capacity with locals and tourists, but the *maître d'hôtel* had obviously been expecting them, and without delay they were shown to a table in an alcove where a bottle of expensive wine was already cooling in a bucket of ice. The *maître d'* lit the candle on their table, and before leaving he summoned a waiter to serve them. They placed their orders after a brief perusal of the menu, then a steward appeared beside their table to pour their wine.

Kerry had been nervous and tense at first, but after a few sips of wine she could feel herself begin to relax, and Max was also such an interesting person to talk to that the next hour and a half passed with unbelievable swiftness.

'I hope you remembered to bring along a good sunshield lotion?' They were drinking their coffee, and the flickering flame of the candle seemed to add a strange fire to his eyes when he unexpectedly reached across the small table to trail the tip of one long finger from her cheekbone down to her chin. 'In the desert areas of this country the sun can ruin a young and pretty face,' he added.

His touch had unnerved her considerably, but she was quick to recover. If he had known her better he would have realised that it was unnecessary to warn her of the hazards of outdoor living, but Kerry left the matter there and steered the conversation back on to an impersonal level.

'I'd like some idea of what's expected of me on this trip.' That hint of sensuality she glimpsed in his smile made her cheeks burn and she added hastily, 'On the photographic side, that is.'

'I'm giving you a free hand in that department, and you may photograph anything of interest that catches your eye as long as it's numbered and the locality listed.' Max observed her intently while he spoke. 'If you're familiar with my work, then it should give you some idea of what I require.'

Kerry did not answer him. She was only too familiar with his work, but she could not decide whether she ought to tell him or keep it to herself.

'You told me that you'd read one of my books,' he persisted with a glimmer of derisive mockery in the eyes that held hers captive. 'Did you actually read the book, or did you just say you did because you felt it was expected of you?'

She no longer had a choice. She could not remain silent and allow him to believe that coming face to face with an author had prompted her to make a polite but untruthful statement.

'I've read all your books,' she confessed.

'All of them?'

'Josie gave me your first book as a birthday gift, and I bought the others as they were published.' The corners of her mouth lifted in amusement at the faintly stunned look that flitted across his face. 'I've read all your books, and some of them I've actually read several times.'

'Do you enjoy reading travelogues?' he asked mockingly, and Kerry rose instantly to the bait.

'Your books aren't mere travelogues,' she protested vehemently. 'When you write about a country you give the reader a very clear insight into the existing political atmosphere. You also acquaint your readers with the people of that nation and their customs, and you do it all in such a way that there have been times when I could have sworn I'd been there myself.'

You've said too much! she told herself. For God's sake, Kerry, did you have to make it so damnably obvious that you're absolutely crazy about his books?

There was an unfathomable expression in the eyes that held hers across the candlelit table. 'I didn't expect such a complimentary reply,' he said, 'but I believe it was sincere, and I thank you for that.'

A strange tension had suddenly developed between them, and Kerry could not find the reason for it. She searched his rugged features in the hope of finding the answer there, but his expression had become shuttered.

'What time do you want to leave in the morning?' she asked when they had finished their coffee.

'I want us to leave immediately after breakfast, and breakfast is at seven in the morning, so I suggest we have an early night.'

He rose from the table as he was speaking, forcing Kerry to do the same, and there was an odd tightness in her throat as they left the restaurant in silence and took the lift up to their rooms on the third floor.

What was wrong? What had she done?

It was after ten-thirty that evening before she got into bed and switched off the light, but she lay awake for a long time trying to find an explanation for Maxwell Harper's abrupt change of mood. Was it something she had said? She had perhaps been a little too dramatic when she had praised his work, but that was not a good enough reason for him to adopt that cool, distant manner.

She sighed heavily and rolled over on to her side so that she could see the night sky through the bedroom window. She was beginning to suspect that Max was a complicated man to understand, and she left it at that when she felt herself drifting off to sleep.

CHAPTER FIVE

THE ivory-coloured Range Rover had been equipped with everything they could possibly require on those nights when they would have to forgo the luxury of a hotel or a rest camp to set up a camp of their own somewhere in the wilds of Namibia.

Kerry could understand why Max had limited her to one suitcase and her camera equipment. There had been no room in the back of the Range Rover for excess baggage, but she had had no cause to complain, since Max had limited himself just as severely. His luggage consisted of a briefcase, a small portable typewriter, and one suitcase which was no bigger than her own.

She had always wondered whether he wrote his books in longhand, but she should have known that he would have mastered the art of using a typewriter after all those years he had spent as a correspondent.

Kerry eased her legs into a more comfortable position and stole a sidelong glance at the silent man seated at the wheel of the well-sprung four-wheel-drive vehicle. She had chosen to wear trousers again, but she was already beginning to regret this decision when she noticed how cool Max looked in a white T-shirt, khaki shorts and brown canvas shoes. He had strong calves to complement his muscled thighs, and against the deeply tanned skin was the shadow of dark, springy hair. Her glance lingered for a moment on that hard thigh nearest her own, but that sudden, compelling desire to touch him made her look away quickly to concentrate on the long, dusty road ahead of them.

Max appeared to be in a better frame of mind this morning, Kerry was thinking. 'I'll stop whenever you want to take photographs,' he had assured her before their departure from the hotel. 'And I don't mind how often or for how long we have to stop.'

Kerry had studied the map he had given her. The zigzag route he had plotted across the country had given her an insight into which areas of Namibia they would be visiting during the next three weeks, and, apart from a few deviations, they would be travelling mainly south on that first day.

After leaving Windhoek that morning they had driven through the foothills of the Khomas Hochland, which, as Max had explained, were one of the main physiographical elements of the central Damaraland highlands.

'The formation you see consists of quartzites and schists,' he explained conversationally when he had to stop once again for Kerry to take photographs. 'It builds a much dissected tableland which rises eventually to an altitude of nearly two thousand metres, and it's from these mountains that the Kuiseb river flows into the Namib desert.'

It was not long before the gravelly road climbed to that dizzy height which Max had mentioned, and, as they drove on, the increasingly rugged countryside began to hold a certain fascination for Kerry. Deep folds incised the arid landscape near the Kuiseb canyon, which cut a decisive rift in the escarpment of the Khomas Hochland, and she could not imagine anything more wild and beautiful.

It was in the blistering midday heat that they reached the shady banks of the dry Tsondab river, and by that time Kerry was convinced she would suffocate if she did not exchange her trousers for something cooler.

Max got out of the Range Rover and laced his fingers behind his head as he stretched to ease the stiffness out of his long body. His T-shirt lifted in the process, exposing a strip of his smoothly tanned back, and when he flexed his leg muscles her attention was drawn to his firm, nicely rounded male buttocks beneath the hip-hugging shorts.

Would he be tanned evenly all over, or would his skin be pale where his swimming-trunks created a barrier against the sun? she wondered.

She wrenched open the door beside her and stepped down on to the gravelly, sun-baked earth, the physical action an extension of the mental effort she was making to rein in her wildly wandering thoughts.

'I must change into something cooler,' she said when Max opened up the back of the vehicle to take out a folded sheet of canvas.

'I wondered how long you'd last in those trousers,' he chuckled throatily as he spread the canvas on the ground beneath the shady acacia tree.

'I didn't think the hotel management would approve if I walked into the dining-room this morning wearing shorts, and we left in such a hurry after breakfast that there wasn't time to change,' she explained as she dragged her suitcase closer and opened it.

She pulled out a pair of shorts which were several shades darker than the blue cotton blouse which was clinging damply to her back. She would have to change in the Range Rover, since the vegetation was too sparse to give her sufficient cover, but the quickest and most comfortable way would be to change where she stood.

Without thinking her hands followed through with the action, but she froze when her fingers touched the metal button at her waist.

What the hell am I doing? she asked herself.

She looked up with a nervous start, and her insides went into a spasm when she saw Max standing a few paces away from her, his arms akimbo and his dark glance resting on her with a great deal of interest.

'Need any help?' he asked, his eyes suddenly issuing a challenge which she could not ignore if she did not want to be made to look and feel a bigger fool than she already believed she was.

Kerry groaned inwardly and cursed herself for being so stupid. She had no choice now; she had to follow through with what she had started so unintentionally.

She had been on many hikes and camping tours in the past where privacy was a commodity which had been sadly lacking. She had adapted to the conditions on those occasions, and she could adapt to it again now, she remonstrated with herself in an attempt to bolster her courage.

It had taken no more than a fraction of a second for these thoughts to flash through her mind, but it felt like hours before she could trust her voice sufficiently to respond to his query.

'I'll manage if you wouldn't mind looking the other way,' she said coolly, and Max lifted one dark eyebrow in a mocking arch.

'Do you expect me to believe you've never taken your clothes off in front of a man before?'

'I have,' she confessed, 'but not when he's stood staring the way you are, and not in broad daylight.'

Make of that what you wish, Maxwell Harper! she thought.

'It appears you prefer the darkness, but there's very little a woman can hide from a man in the darkness,' he continued to mock her while he obligingly turned his back on her. 'Your clothes don't hide the fact that you have a beautiful figure, and from the first moment I saw you in my sister's house I've been convinced that you have a delightful body which would be as pleasing on the eye as it would be to the touch.'

If this was an attempt to unnerve her, then Max had succeeded admirably. Her fingers had fumbled with the metal button and the zip after he had turned his broad back on her, but now her legs felt so unsteady beneath her that she was in danger of losing her balance when she peeled off her trousers.

'Have I shocked you with my revelations?' he asked with a hint of laughter in his voice when she remained silent.

Kerry's heart was thudding against her ribs as she snatched up her shorts and stepped into them. 'Do you think we could change the subject?' she said shortly.

'Why?' he demanded with a throaty, almost sensual chuckle. 'Don't you like the idea that I've tried to imagine what you'd look like without your clothes?'

'No, I don't.'

'Haven't you imagined the same about me?'

'No!' Her denial echoed falsely in her own ears as she recalled the naked thoughts she had entertained some minutes earlier when she had admired his posterior.

'Liar,' he accused over one broad shoulder, and the stinging heat that surged into her cheeks had nothing to do with the warmth of the Namibian sun on her face. 'May I turn round now?'

'Yes, you may,' she said, snapping down the catches of her suitcase and leaning into the back of the Range Rover to return it to its original position.

Her back had been turned to Max, but she felt him coming up behind her, and her heart was suddenly hammering so loudly in her breast that she was convinced he must hear it.

'Hm... nice legs,' he observed when she straightened from her task, and she despised herself as she once again felt that wave of embarrassing heat surging into her cheeks.

'Is that our lunch?' she asked, attempting to divert his attention with her unnecessary query and gesturing towards the two disposable polystyrene containers he was holding in his hands.

'You know it is.' He stacked the one container on top of the other and cupped her chin firmly in his free hand so that she was forced to meet the probing intensity of his faintly mocking glance. 'For a woman of twenty-six you still appear to blush easily, Kerry Ann Nelson, and I'm intrigued. I want to know more about you—much, *much* more—and I suspect I will before we come to the end of this trip.'

The connotation was intimate, making her stiffen with resentment, and he released her with a placating smile as if he could sense the alarm spiralling through her.

'Let's eat,' he said abruptly, thrusting a container into her hands and turning away to lower his long, muscular body on to the canvas he had spread out beneath the tree.

Kerry expelled the air slowly from her tortured lungs, unaware that she had scarcely breathed until she experienced that giddy sensation of someone who had held his or her breath for too long a period. She managed to look outwardly calm when she followed him down on to the canvas, but her legs were still shaking, and she seated herself awkwardly. She had not thought about food all morning, and when she opened the container she was balancing on her thighs she could not honestly say she was hungry.

The hotel had packed a light lunch of spicy chicken portions, fresh bread rolls, a salad and a small carton of fruit juice. It had been prepared and arranged in the container with such obvious care that Kerry felt compelled to make an attempt at eating somc of it.

'I didn't realise how hungry I was until I started eating,' Max remarked conversationally, breaking the lengthy silence that had settled between them.

Kerry looked up to see him biting into a piece of chicken with his strong white teeth, and when she lowered her gaze to the container in her lap she couldn't curb the surprised, faintly self-conscious laugh that burst past her lips.

'Neither did I,' she confessed, surveying the remnants of a meal which she had believed she could not do justice to.

'You have a nice laugh, Kerry. I think you should try to relax and laugh more often instead of taking everything so seriously.'

Kerry chose not to comment on that statement. How could she tell him that she found it impossible trying to relax in his presence while every nerve and sinew in her body was constantly flaring in an unwanted, embarrassing response to his maleness? No, she could never tell him that, she decided, shrinking inwardly at the mere idea while they finished their lunch in a silence dominated by the shrill, singing call of the cicadas in the trees.

She narrowed her eyes against the white-hot glare of the sun as she stared out across the dry river-bed, and could not help wondering if the parched earth had ever known the luxury of a soaking rush of water.

'Does it ever rain in this part of the country?' she asked, glancing briefly at Max while she tucked a stray strand of hair behind her left ear.

'They get the occasional hard downpour,' he explained, directing his own narrowed gaze out across the river-bed and beyond. 'The grasses in this area die off when the soil dries out, but their seeds lie dormant until the next rain. The succulents store moisture in their stems or in their leaves, and larger plants, like the camelthorn trees, send their roots up to fifteen metres down to tap the soil water table which gives them a continuous supply of water even in a drought.'

Kerry collected her cameras and went for a short walk along the banks of the dry river. Before they left this particular part of the country she had to capture on film the stark reality of a merciless sun beating down on a parched earth from a blue, cloudless sky.

Max took a route past some of the most spectacular dunes of the Namib desert. It was late afternoon and they were seventy-two kilometres south-west of Maltahöhe before he stopped again in the deserted parking area of a castle which stood on a hill overlooking the barren landscape that surrounded it.

'This is Schloss Duwisib,' he said as they got out of the Range Rover.

Kerry looked up at the castle, her gaze shifting from the central tower and corner turrets to the loopholes built into the massive stone walls. The structure looked solid and impregnable, and she wondered how long it had stood there like a fortress against the harsh elements of nature.

'The Duwisib castle was built in 1908,' Max answered Kerry's unspoken query. 'The original owner was a Baron Hans Heinrich von Wolf, and I was told he erected the castle at a cost of some twenty-five thousand pounds. He furnished it extravagantly, and lived here for about five years with his American wife before he returned to Germany where he was reinstated in the army, but a year later he was killed in action in Flanders.'

'How sad,' she murmured, her eyes clouding, but she controlled herself and hastily prepared her Leica to take a few photographs before the light faded. 'Is the castle still privately owned?'

'It belongs to a company that's built it up into an extremely successful Karakul sheep-breeding station, and they've also gone to great lengths to preserve the castle and its contents in their original state.' Max waited with admirable patience while Kerry photographed the castle from various angles. 'Shall we take a quick look inside before they close the doors on us?' he asked when she was finished.

'I'd like that.'

'Come along, then, and hurry,' he instructed, taking her hand in a firm grip and almost dragging her at a running pace up the wide path towards the tree-sheltered entrance.

It was pleasantly cool inside the stone walls of the castle, but the fireplaces which had been built into most of the rooms suggested that it could become bitterly cold during the winter months.

The twenty-two rooms, arranged in a U-shape, housed a unique collection of furniture and fine portraits, and an interesting array of weapons from the seventeenth and eighteenth centuries. It needed to be viewed at one's leisure, but Max's whirlwind tour had been long enough to give Kerry a glimpse into the castle's illustrious past when Baron von Wolf had lived there with his wife in true aristocratic style.

Kerry wished they could have stayed a while longer, but the doorman had been jiggling his bunch of keys impatiently for a considerable length of time before they vacated the castle to travel on to Maltahöhe, where Max had planned they would spend the night.

Their accommodation for that evening was not of the same calibre as the hotel in Windhoek, but Kerry had no cause for complaint. The room was clean, the bed felt comfortable enough, and she had a bathroom to herself in which she could soak away the dust she had collected during the first long, hot day on the road with Max.

The dining-room had offered a wholesome, pre-set menu. It had started with a creamy German-style pea soup and had ended with a marvellous strawberry dessert served with ice-cream. Every dish had been tastefully prepared, and Kerry had eaten so much that she felt too lazy to be anything but relaxed when they were finishing off their meal with a small cup of black, aromatic coffee.

Her glance collided with Max's across the small table, and he was observing her with such an odd expression in his eyes that it aroused a faint stab of uneasiness. 'Why are you looking at me like that?' she asked.

'I've just realised something I never stopped to consider before.' His dark glance dipped briefly to the creamy smoothness of her shoulders beneath the pencil-thin straps of her silky black dress, then he looked up again and smiled apologetically. 'You're an attractive and intelligent woman, Kerry, and I'm convinced I'm not the first man to have noticed these qualities, but because of my determination to get you to agree to this assignment I selfishly neglected to ask if I might be inconveniencing someone by taking you away with me for three weeks.'

His admission was oddly touching, but Kerry was not ignorant of the fact that this was also a calculated attempt on his behalf to discover whether she had a lover waiting for her in Johannesburg, and the corners of her mouth lifted in amusement at the thought of what Josie would say if she could hear this conversation.

'You've inconvenienced quite a few of my clients, but no one else in particular,' she assured him calmly.

Disbelief flashed across his ruggedly handsome face. 'There must surely be at least *one* man in your life who means more to you than all the rest?'

Kerry's candid glance did not waver from his as she shook her head. 'I have a few male acquaintances, and I enjoy their company on a professional basis, but there's no one special in my life.'

'Is this by chance or design?' he demanded, his eyes narrowed and his expression unfathomable.

'It's a bit of both, I would say,' she smiled wryly. 'I lead a full and reasonably active life, but at twenty-six I've already become too set in my ways to want to rush headlong into any kind of relationship with a man without stopping to consider all the various aspects of such an action.'

'There must have been someone special once,' he said, looking at her long and hard.

'What makes you think that?'

Max's sensuous mouth curved mockingly. 'You weren't always twenty-six and too set in your ways to rush headlong into a relationship with a man, so I'm assuming that there was someone once. Am I right?'

Kerry looked away towards the far end of the room and focused her attention for a moment on a group of tourists discussing their itinerary over dinner.

'Yes, you're right,' she said at length. 'There was someone once, and the relationship was quite serious for a while.'

'What happened?'

She smiled with unaccustomed cynicism as she met Max's probing glance across the table. 'He forgot to tell me he already had a wife and three children.'

'Nasty,' he commented.

'It *was* nasty, and it will be a long time before I allow myself to become seriously involved with a man again,' she assured him.

'When you talk about having a serious relationship with a man, then I presume you'd want it to include the possibility of marriage.'

'I'm not anywhere near the desperate stage yet, but I'd like to get married some day,' she answered him cautiously. 'Wouldn't you?'

'No, I wouldn't.' His reply was emphatic and it was delivered without the slightest hesitation. 'I've always enjoyed my nomadic existence. I find it personally as well as professionally satisfying, and I also realised a long time ago that my choice of career would never be able to accommodate a wife and family. There are very few women who'd be happy with a husband who spent six to nine months of every year away from home, and if we happened to have children I wouldn't like to think that I'd robbed them of a stable home life by never being there for them when I was needed.'

This was the clarity Kerry had sought. This was what that look on his face had meant when he had spoken about his photographer friend having to curtail his activities since his wife had had a child. She understood his reasoning perhaps better than anyone else. She knew what it felt like to grow up without a father in the home, and Max knew it too. Why, then, did it hurt so much?

'Do you ever get lonely?' she asked, and he smiled derisively.

'Loneliness is a state of mind that lends itself to inactivity.'

'You could be actively involved with something in a room filled with all your friends and acquaintances and you could still experience that feeling of loneliness, Max,' she told him.

The mockery in his smile deepened as he waved aside her argument. 'I consider that an extreme improbability.'

Kerry was in a curiously disturbed frame of mind when they retired to their rooms, and she lay awake for a long time that night. She was thinking about Max and the conversation they had had, and she suspected he could be brutally honest about what he wanted. Max was different from any man she had ever known, but he was also just as unobtainable.

'Kerry, you're a prize idiot!' she muttered fiercely into the darkness. 'First you get yourself mixed up with a man who's already married, and now you're allowing yourself to become attracted to a man who's ruled marriage out of his life. Well, it seems that when it comes to men you certainly know how to pick the ones who are beyond your reach!'

Sleep did not come easily after that, and she spent a restless night tossing and turning on her bed. It showed the following morning, but if Max noticed then he tactfully refrained from mentioning it.

Kerry realised that there was only one way she could survive the next few weeks. Her attitude had to remain businesslike and her thoughts had to be centred solely on her job; but that was not so easy, with Max always so close at hand to disturb her concentration with his nearness.

He took an active interest in what she was doing, and he would often draw her attention to something which he thought might interest her. He would relate many of the historical facts, or regale her with interesting and amusing anecdotes, but somehow their conversations would always veer towards the personal, and that was what Kerry was trying so desperately to avoid.

They spent three full days in Lüderitz, a town with a melancholy charm which lay nestled in a bay on the rocky south coast of Namibia. The fishing fleets and canning factories had dwindled to a few, but this coastal town was still at the centre of a flourishing rock lobster industry, and Kerry spent a few interesting hours at the harbour with Max, taking candid photographs of the fishermen as they hauled in their catch.

There was so much to see and photograph in and around Lüderitz, and Max had planned a rigorous itinerary which left them with very little time for relaxation.

It was not until their last day that they found time to drive out to Kolmanskop—that fascinating ghost town where the first diamonds had been mined, and they arrived there in the afternoon when it was free of tourists.

They parked the Range Rover to explore the area on foot, and Max waved his arm in an encompassing gesture. 'No one has lived here since 1956,' he said.

That much was obvious to Kerry. Over the years the old, abandoned buildings had been ravaged by the sand and the desert winds until they had become a part of the insidiously shifting dunes.

The whine of the sharp breeze was in her ears, adding to the eeriness of the experience as they moved about among the ruins of those once magnificent buildings and surveyed the scattered debris of rusted machinery which had become partially buried by the shifting sands. It was sad, but it was sadder still to think that these weeks with Max were also destined to lie forgotten beneath the sands of time.

'You're trembling.' Max placed an arm about her shoulders, drawing her against his side, and the smell of the sun on his body mingled pleasantly with the scent of his woody cologne. 'There's an aura about this place that often affects people this way.'

'I'm all right,' she said, wishing he would let her go when the feel of that hard body against her own made her nerves flare in alarm.

'You're such a sensitive creature, Kerry.' His strong fingers were beneath her chin, tilting her head back so that she was forced to look up at him, and his face was suddenly so close to hers that she could see the flecks of gold in his brown eyes. 'Are you sure you're all right?'

'Yes, I'm sure, Max.'

There was something else besides concern in his dark appraisal, and for one heart-stopping instant she felt certain that he was going to kiss her, but then he let her go.

Had she imagined it?

Kerry had no desire to dwell on that subject, and she was glad that she was eventually too busy doing the job Max had hired her for to think of anything else.

That evening, after dinner, she went to bed and waited for the familiar sound of Max's typewriter, but she waited in vain. The silence in the adjoining room became vaguely disturbing and she had difficulty falling asleep, but she was drifting off an hour later when the sound of shattering glass jolted her awake.

It had come from Max's room, and she leapt out of bed with a horrifying mental vision of Max lying unconscious on the floor and perhaps bleeding to death. She pulled on her cotton robe as she ran from her room to hammer on his door, and she was still busy tying the belt about her waist when the door was jerked open.

'I heard glass breaking. What happened? Are you hurt?' The words tumbled from her lips in a rush of anxiety while her eyes searched frantically for signs of an injury and found none.

'I knocked the glass off the bedside cupboard in the dark—and no, I haven't hurt myself.'

Relief made way for the ridiculous as she stood there in the deserted hotel corridor staring up at Max with eyes that were still heavy with sleep. She could imagine what she must look like in her faded cotton robe with her feet bare and her hair hanging in a dishevelled state about her face, but she forgot about her own appearance as her mind registered the fact that Max was wearing black jogging shorts and nothing else. His tanned, muscle-toned body suggested a regular work-out in a gym, but he was not bulky like a body-builder. The dark matting of hair on his broad chest trailed down into a V across his flat stomach, and her eyes followed it down to where it disappeared beneath the elastic band of his shorts.

'I'm sorry,' she muttered, sucking in air as she experienced the curious sensation that she had come close to drowning. 'I heard the glass shattering and I was afraid you might have injured yourself. It was silly of me.'

Kerry was backing away apologetically when a long, muscular arm shot out and steely fingers gripped her wrist. She was jerked into the room and the door was closed behind her in a simultaneous action before she was caught up in the hard circle of his arms and being kissed in a way that made her wonder if the world was suddenly spinning off its axis.

It had happened too fast to prevent it, and neither could she halt her own flaring senses. She was kissing him back with a passion she could not control, and when he finally released her she staggered back a few paces to seek the solid support of the wall against her back until that odd, boneless sensation began to ease out of her legs.

The remembered heat of his hard body still seemed to scorch her through the thin cotton of her robe, her palms were tingling in the aftermath of their contact with his bare, muscled flesh, and the intoxicating taste of his mouth was still on her tongue as she tilted her head back to look up at him confusedly.

'Why did you do that?' she croaked.

His smile was derisive, and his eyes, almost black in the dimly lit room, were burning down into hers. 'Wasn't that what you really came for?'

Kerry paled visibly. A slap in the face could not have been more sobering, and the sting of it seemed to reach right down into the core of her being.

'You disappoint me, Max.' The words came awkwardly over her stiff lips while the icy blue of her eyes was the only splash of colour in her ashen face. 'I never imagined you'd be the kind of man who'd fail to recognise genuine concern when you saw it.'

Max did not stop her when she stormed out of his room to return to her own, but his twisted, derisive smile had not escaped her notice, and it was burning its way into her brain until it felt as if it would become branded there for life. It haunted Kerry, and it hurt almost as much as his supposition that she had gone to his room for reasons other than concern. She had meant it when she had said she was disappointed in him, but now that she was alone again she began to wonder about it.

Max had behaved oddly. He was much too shrewd and alert to be fooled by anyone after all those years of being trained to recognise the truth when he saw it. If he had been blind to the truth in this instance, then it had been deliberate, and Kerry wished she could understand the reason for it.

CHAPTER SIX

MAX pulled the Range Rover to the side of the gravel road and brought the vehicle to a skidding halt in a cloud of swirling dust, but he did not switch off the engine.

They had left Lüderitz after breakfast that morning, and they had been travelling for almost four hours in a strained silence which had been broken only by Kerry's periodic requests for him to stop when she had wanted to take photographs.

This time Max was not stopping at Kerry's request, and she directed a quick, curious glance at his rugged profile. A tiny nerve was jumping in his strong jaw as he sat staring straight ahead of him with his hands clenched on the steering-wheel, and she already knew him well enough to recognise the fact that he was agitated about something.

Kerry waited, not knowing what to expect, and a few tense seconds elapsed before he turned his head to pin her to her seat with his dark, penetrating gaze.

'About last night, Kerry.' His glance skimmed briefly over her hair, which she had tied up into a makeshift knot. 'I was way out of line, and I owe you an apology.'

An apology was the last thing she had expected, and her charitable nature leapt instantly to the fore. 'I suspect you were tired and perhaps not in a very good mood, so...' she gestured dismissively and smiled '... apology accepted.'

An unfathomable expression flitted across his face, and he turned slightly in his seat to face her. 'I've never met a woman before who could accept an apology without demanding an explanation. 'You're a rarity, Kerry,' he concluded, brushing the backs of his fingers lightly across her cheek. 'You're a beautiful, rational, sensitive-natured rarity.'

He shifted the Range Rover into gear and drove on, saving Kerry the effort of having to formulate a glib response to his flattering appraisal.

She felt uncomfortable and rather embarrassed. If she was called on to be truthful, then she would have to admit that she *was* curious to know what had motivated his actions and his reasoning the previous evening. Was Max perhaps aware of this? Was he testing her? she wondered as they drove on past low sand dunes covered sparsely with tufts of Bushman grass.

She shook herself mentally. She was becoming much too curious about Max, and if she did not exercise more caution in future then her curiosity might steer her into the very situation she had wanted to avoid.

Further south, en route to the Fish River Canyon, they passed several Karakul breeding stations, and Max discussed with Kerry the intricacies of this thriving industry in which new-born lambs were slaughtered for their silken pelts.

'Namibia exports about three and a half million pelts annually,' he ended their discussion with a statistic.

Poor lambs, Kerry was thinking, and shuddered inwardly when she tried to imagine herself wearing a Swakara coat.

It was early afternoon, but they were already hot and tired when they entered the Fish River Canyon reserve from the north. The popular Ai-Ais hot springs resort was closed during the summer months because of the intense heat and the threat of flash-floods, but Max had obtained a permit giving them permission to set up camp for the night along the eastern ridge of the canyon.

In the shimmering heat of the day there was a certain rugged beauty in the desolation surrounding the deep gorges and fluted chasms of this magnificent structure which nature had created, and Kerry was impatient to capture it on film when Max parked the Range Rover in a spot which he considered suitable for a camping site.

'If you'd like to take a look around, then go ahead while I pitch the tents,' he suggested when they had off-loaded the camping equipment.

'I'll help you set up camp before I go,' she offered.

Max studied her with a dubious and faintly mocking expression in his eyes. 'Do you know anything about pitching tents?'

'Try me,' she challenged, wiping her damp palms against the seat of her khaki shorts.

Half an hour later they were perspiring freely in the blistering sun, but the two tents had been erected and pegged down securely. They would have to crouch to enter their tents, but the interior was large enough to accommodate an inflatable mattress while still leaving them sufficient room to move about.

'If you were a Girl Guide, you'd have earned yourself a badge, but in the circumstances I'll have to reward you like this.' His arm circled her waist, and before she could stop him he had tipped her face up to his to kiss her gently but firmly on the lips. 'You're pretty good, Kerry.'

'At pitching a tent, or kissing?'

Kerry's flushed cheeks went several shades redder the instant those words left her lips. What had possessed her to say something like that? She had been flustered by his kiss and the damp heat of his hard male body against her own, but that was no excuse for her behaviour. Her query had been provocative, and the devilish gleam in Max's eyes told her that he was not going to let her get away with it.

'I think I can vouch for the fact that you're good at both,' he said, his arm tightening about her slim waist and his fingers sliding round to the sensitive nape of her neck. 'I'll have to kiss you again before I can decide which you're best at.'

It was a strange mixture of fear and excitement that held Kerry captive. She could have twisted free of Max's grasp, but instead her hands were fluttering ineffectually against his broad chest while she stood paralysed by her own conflicting emotions.

'I'm sorry, Max, but I wasn't——'

Kerry's belated attempt at an explanatory protest was stifled by his sensuous mouth shifting over hers. She stood rigid at first, fighting desperately against the more natural urge to respond, but her resistance faltered and then crumbled dangerously when Max skilfully coaxed her lips apart with his tongue.

She was sliding out of her depth and rapidly losing control as he invaded the sweet, moist warmth of her mouth. The intimacy of his kisses was beginning to intoxicate her, and she was driven by an urgency she had never known before as she leaned into him and laced her fingers together at the back of his dark head.

Max's hands shifted down along her back to clasp her firm, shapely bottom and, encouraged by her response, he drew her closer into the curve of his aroused body until her hips and thighs were moulded firmly to his.

Time was being measured by heartbeats and desire was setting a wild pace that left Kerry teetering helplessly on the brink of something she could only guess at when

Max finally eased his mouth from hers to seek out that frantic little pulse at the base of her throat.

The sun was hot against her closed eyelids, but it was nothing compared to the heated pleasure aroused by Max's touch when he shifted his hands up beneath her T-shirt to stroke her breasts through her satiny bra and rake his thumbs across their hardening peaks.

Kerry stiffened against him, startled by the intimacy of his touch and alarmed by the strength of her own physical response to it.

This has got to stop, she was thinking as his strong, lean fingers trailed an erotic path along her spine to awaken her to the devastation of sensations she had never experienced before.

She was allowing herself to be drawn deeper into something she did not want, something which she knew she did not have the ability to deal with, but Max's sensuous mouth was shifting over hers again, demanding a response she could not withhold, and that warning little voice at the back of her mind was temporarily silenced.

'I can't decide which you're best at,' Max announced throatily when he eventually lifted his mouth from hers. 'You'd be an asset when it comes to pitching tents, but I suspect a man would be more inclined to want to become addicted to your kisses.'

Kerry was not listening to what he was saying. She was finding it difficult trying to surface from that well of emotions she had been plunged into, but while she did so her palms were acquainting themselves with the fact that Max's heart was beating as uncontrollably hard and fast as her own. He lowered his head to claim her lips again, but she had had enough time to regain control of herself, and she was thinking sanely again when she used her hands as leverage against his chest to evade his plundering mouth.

'I think this situation is getting out of hand,' she said, her voice surprisingly calm, but not quite as steady as she would have wished.

'I think you may be right,' he agreed, releasing her with a glint of mockery in his eyes, and a few embarrassing seconds elapsed before he turned from her to point at something off to her right. 'If you take a walk beyond that quiver tree you should have an excellent view of the canyon, but I must warn you not to venture too close to the edge. The terrain can be treacherous in places.'

Kerry's legs felt horribly unsteady beneath her, and her heart was still pounding uncomfortably hard against her ribs when she turned without speaking and walked away from him to collect her camera equipment.

She was also angry with herself as she recalled the careless ease with which she had placed herself in jeopardy. If this was how she was going to cope with the attraction, she felt sorry for herself.

The quiver tree Max had pointed out was some distance away from the camp, but when Kerry stepped beyond it she forgot about everything except the magnificence of the natural wonder that lay at her feet. Range after folding range lay spread out before her, and this awe-inspiring view continued for almost as far as her eyes could see.

She selected a spot from which to take photographs, and she stayed there for the remainder of the afternoon, seated beneath a shady umbrella with her cameras at the ready. She was fascinated by the ever-changing perspective of the canyon with the varying intensity of light and moving shadows, and she was thrilled that she had been in no hurry to leave when, as evening approached, she saw the folding ranges turn to an incredible turquoise-blue with deep, dark shadows.

She was loath to return to the camp after what had occurred between Max and herself, but it was already long after seven and she did not relish the thought that he might think it necessary to come searching for her. She sighed as she gathered up her equipment, and the sun was still hovering on the western horizon like a flaming red ball in the sky when she hoisted the folded umbrella over her shoulder and walked back to the camp.

Max was seated at a small fold-up table beneath the canvas awning at the entrance to his tent, and he was hammering away at the keys of his portable typewriter when Kerry approached the camp. His hands stilled abruptly on the keys when he heard her footsteps crunching on the gravelly earth, and he looked up sharply.

'Please continue while the light is still good,' she said apologetically, his frowning glance making her suspect that he had not welcomed the intrusion on his thoughts. 'I'll see what I can do about making us something to eat.'

A strange expression flitted across his rugged face as he continued to stare at her, and she was beginning to think he had not heard a word she had said when he inclined his head briefly and carried on working.

Kerry stored her camera equipment in her tent and washed her hot face and dusty hands in a small basin of water before she started to prepare their meal.

She worked in a silence broken only by the staccato sound of the typewriter's keys and the hissing flame of the gas cooker, but while she worked she found her glance straying constantly in Max's direction. If only she could pretend that nothing unusual had happened between them and that everything was still as it had been before, but that was not possible.

The game of pretence was for children, not adults, Kerry remonstrated with herself. She had to face the truth instead of wanting to hide from it. She glanced briefly at Max and looked away again. They had ignited a passion in each other which was not going to be written off as easily as the incident in his hotel room the night before, and neither could she ignore the fact that she had responded to his kisses with an eagerness that made her cringe with shame whenever she recalled those moments.

There was no way she could erase the memory of what had occurred between them, but she was going to do everything within her power to make sure that it never happened again.

She was buttering bread rolls in the swiftly fading light when Max packed away his typewriter and carried the small table across to where she was working. He lit the gas lamp and laid the table without speaking, but Kerry could feel the emotional vibrations between them, and it unnerved her.

'This smells good,' he remarked when they sat down to eat, and his heavy eyebrows rose a fraction in surprise after the first mouthful. 'It tastes good too. What is it?'

'It's nothing terribly elaborate. I opened a few cans to concoct a stew, but if you want the recipe then I'm afraid you'll have to read the labels on the cans.'

He looked up from his plate and his mouth twitched in response to that twinkle of humour he had glimpsed in her eyes. 'You're a remarkable young woman, Kerry Nelson, and I'm beginning to wonder how many surprises you still have in store for me before this trip comes to an end.'

The smile faded abruptly from Kerry's eyes. 'I'm used to the outdoor life, and I'm not trying to surprise you or impress you in any way.'

'Did I give the impression that I thought that of you?' he asked.

'No, you didn't.' Her smile was strained. 'I just wanted to make sure there wouldn't be any misunderstandings on the subject.'

'Understood.' His response was curt, then his strong white teeth flashed in a bone-melting smile. 'You're taking everything too seriously, Kerry. Just enjoy yourself, and relax.'

Relax? Kerry wanted to laugh a little hysterically. How could she relax when it took so little effort to recall every embarrassing detail of what had occurred between them? And how could she relax when a part of her was beginning to crave a repetition?

They finished off their meal with a cup of coffee, and afterwards Max helped Kerry with the dishes. She washed and he dried, and when everything was packed away tidily he sat down again beside the gas lamp to read through the pages he had typed earlier.

It was too early to go to bed, so Kerry decided to leave Max with his work while she went for a short walk. The moon was full, lighting her path, and somehow she found herself retracing her steps to the spot she had occupied for most of that afternoon.

The view of the canyon by the light of the full moon was spectacular, and Kerry drew an audible breath as she seated herself on a low, flat boulder. Nothing seemed to stir while she sat staring out across the canyon, and she could almost make herself believe she had been transported back in time to an age long before life had existed on this earth. An immense silence permeated her senses, and in the depths below her the ghostly shadows seemed to speak of aeons of lifeless antiquity.

She could not recall afterwards how long she had sat there in mesmerised fascination before the sound of a shoe crunching on gravel brought her sharply back to the present, and she glanced nervously over her shoulder to see Max walking towards her.

'It's beautiful by moonlight, isn't it?' he said, straddling the narrow boulder behind her and filling her with alarm when she found herself perched between his powerful thighs; but he didn't touch her.

'Beautiful,' she agreed distractedly, forcing herself to remain seated despite the disquieting heat of his body against her back.

'The bushmen like to believe that the canyon was once the lair of Kouteign Koorou, and that it was the violent rage of this serpent from the distant past that caused the deep, ragged twists in the canyon.'

His warm breath fanned the fine hair at the nape of her neck when he spoke, and the deep velvet of his voice sent little tremors of unwanted pleasure darting through her.

'The monster was apparently desperate to escape the relentless pursuit of the hunters,' Max went on to explain, 'and as it retreated into the desert it gouged deep scars into the land in its efforts to evade its tormenters.'

'It always amazes me how the indigenous races of Africa so often have a mythical explanation for the existence of a geographic phenomenon.' Kerry looked up at the star-studded night sky and smiled at the memory of some of her own amusing experiences. 'The Kore-Kore tribe of Zimbabwe believe that the stars are torches carried by the good spirits as they go about their work.'

'Zimbabwe's a fascinating country. Have you been there?'

'Only on a brief visit.' As the silence lengthened between them Kerry was taunted by the memory of her eager response to Max's kisses, and when she felt him stir behind her she could not stop herself from leaping nervously to her feet. 'It's getting late. I think I'll go back to the camp.'

'You can run away from me, Kerry, but you can't run away from yourself,' he said as if he had read her thoughts. 'What happened this afternoon was something we both wanted,' he added as he got to his feet, 'and neither of us can guarantee that we won't find a way to make it happen again.'

'I don't... I don't want it to—to happen again.'

'Don't you?'

No, I don't! She wanted to shout that denial at him, but she couldn't. Her heart was beating somewhere in her throat, blocking the passage of that lie before it could reach her lips, because she was suddenly besieged by an intense longing to lose herself in his arms and his kisses.

He lifted his hand, his fingers touching a silvery strand of hair which had escaped the tight coil in her neck, and, frightened by the intensity of that yearning to be closer to him, she shrank away.

'Kerry...'

'Don't touch me!' she croaked, backing away from his hands as he reached for her, and suddenly the gravelly soil was giving way beneath her feet.

Icy fear shot through her as she realised that she was teetering on the sloping edge of the canyon, but the scream of terror that rose in her throat never materialised. Steely hands yanked her back to safety, and she landed against Max's solid chest with a thud that almost robbed her of breath. She was shaking uncontrollably, and the aching numbness of relief surging into her limbs almost made her collapse in a heap at his feet.

'For the love of God, Kerry!' he groaned into her hair. 'You could have killed yourself!'

'I'm sorry, it—it was stupid of me,' she muttered, shuddering inwardly as she freed herself from his steadying hands, and before he could say anything else she turned and ran back to the camp at a stumbling, frantic pace, as if Kouteign Koorou himself were following hard on her heels.

Kerry had washed and changed in the dark, and was crawling into her sleeping-bag when she heard Max returning to the camp. Shock was taking its toll, and she was shaking so badly that she had to clench her jaw to stop her teeth from chattering when the tent flap was lifted and a torch was shone into her face.

She bolted up into a sitting position and dragged the folds of the sleeping-bag around her as she blinked into that piercing beam. 'Who's that?' she demanded.

As if she didn't know!

'You know damn well it's me, Kerry!' Max responded tersely to her stupid query.

'What—what do you want?'

The beam of the torch was directed elsewhere, and her heart was thudding painfully against her ribs when Max eased himself into the tent. He knelt on the ground sheet beside the mattress, and only then did she see the glass of amber liquid in his hand.

'Drink this,' he instructed, putting the torch aside and holding the glass so close to her nose that she could not fail to identify the contents.'

'I don't drink brandy,' she said.

'You'd better drink it, Kerry, or I swear I'll pour it forcibly down your throat!'

She did not doubt him. In her highly sensitised state of shock she could feel the aggression emanating from him, but her hand was shaking so violently that his fingers had to retain their grip on the glass to steady it for her.

She drew a choking breath, then coughed as the first mouthful of the stinging liquid hit the unsuspecting walls of her stomach. Max was urging her to drink it all, but halfway through she felt like gagging.

'That's enough, Max. Please—no more,' she begged, shuddering visibly at the mere smell of the brandy.

'How do you feel now?' he asked.

'Much better, thank you.' The heat in her stomach was spreading swiftly into her veins, easing the tremors that shock had aroused, but Max continued to eye her doubtfully. 'I'm fine,' she added, wishing he would go before that irrational longing returned to make her blunder foolishly into another near-fatal situation. 'Really I am.'

His steady regard was beginning to unnerve her when he bunched his fist into the hair at the nape of her neck and dragged her face close to his.

'You're a disrupting influence in my life,' he said with a harsh note of anger in his voice. 'I was lying awake last night, and I was thinking about you, when I accidentally knocked the glass off the bedside cupboard, but the last thing I expected was to find the object of my thoughts hammering at my door. I knew you were there because you were concerned that I might have injured myself, but at that precise moment your state of dishevelled femininity was a torment I could have done without.'

'I'm sorry, Max, I——'

'I wanted you last night.'

'Don't say that!' she gasped.

'It's the truth! I've been wanting you more and more every day we've been together, but I can't overlook the fact that I forced you to accept this assignment. I've done my damnedest to control my feelings because I could imagine what you might think, but I wasn't having much success last night, and that made me angry.'

'So you looked for an excuse to lash out at me.'

'That's the part I've regretted most.' He was drawing her closer, tilting her face up to his, and her blue eyes widened in alarm when she felt his warm breath on her mouth. Max saw that look, and released her, with an angry expletive on his lips, to sit back on his heels. 'What is it that you're afraid of, Kerry?' he asked quietly.

Kerry had never quite mastered the art of evading the truth, and with all that brandy inside her it seemed so much simpler to opt for honesty.

'I've admired your work for a long time, Max, and now I've learned to respect you as a person.' She raised her hands, palms upwards, in a pleading gesture. 'I know I can't run away from what happened between us this afternoon, but it made me realise how quickly a silly situation could erupt into something that I couldn't control, and I—I don't want us to do anything that might spoil our existing relationship.'

'Something sparked between us the first time we met,' he told her, 'and don't tell me you didn't feel it.'

'I felt it, and that's really why I was so adamant about not accepting this assignment. I was afraid I wouldn't be able to cope with my feelings if I had to spend so much time alone with you.' Understanding flickered in his dark eyes, but his face retained that harsh look in the torchlight, and her courage almost deserted her. 'I don't want to have a casual affair with you, Max,' she added quietly. 'There'd be no future in it for me.'

He fingered his square jaw as if she had delivered an unexpected blow. 'Does there have to be a future?'

'Yes. If I'm going to lay my feelings on the altar of a relationship with a man, then I must have some indication that it might lead to something permanent.'

A mirthless smile curved her soft mouth during the ensuing silence. Now he knew it all. There could be no misunderstandings and no recriminations now that they both knew exactly where they stood.

'I appreciate your honesty, Kerry, and I'll respect your wishes,' he said at length, his deep voice drained of the rasping aggression he had displayed earlier. 'I think you know as well as I do that I could never give you what you would expect from a relationship. I've told you before, I need my freedom, so—for both our sakes—I think we should make an effort to stick to the rules of a business relationship.'

Kerry lay awake for a long time after he had gone, but the immense silence—and the brandy—finally worked on her like a drug. She went to sleep, but her dreams were filled with thrashing monsters and gaping chasms. Max was there in all her dreams, offering her the safety of his strength, but when she awoke the following morning she knew that the *real* nightmare had been in the latter part of her dreams.

Max would not always be there for her. When this assignment was over he would walk out of her life in much the same way he had walked into it, and that was something Kerry knew she would be wise to remember.

CHAPTER SEVEN

THE afternoon heat was oppressive, and Kerry was seated beneath a leafy acacia tree, trying to cool herself with the plaited grass fan she had bought from an old Herero woman near Gobabis. Max had taken off his T-shirt while he changed the fan belt on the Range Rover, and her appreciative glance lingered for a moment on the rippling muscles in his back and powerful arms, but her mind was reflecting on what she had encountered during the two weeks since they had left the Fish River Canyon.

It had taken ten days and almost two thousand gruelling kilometres of stop-start motoring to reach Tsumeb in the north. After two days of comfortable living in one of the local hotels they had travelled west again through the Etosha National Park to the old German fort near Sesfontein in the Kaoko Veld.

They were heading south again on the final leg of their journey back to Windhoek, and soon—much too soon—they would be saying goodbye to this extraordinary country to return to Johannesburg.

Kerry screwed up her eyes against the glare of the sun and sighed ruefully as she stared out across the sun-baked Damaraland plains.

Heat, dust, and magnificent scenery—those words were synonymous when describing Namibia. It was also a country of wide expanses, mystical sunrises and spectacular sunsets.

There was more to it than that, she was thinking as she leaned forward to watch the tedious progress of a dung beetle rolling a large ball of dung to its burial ground. Namibia was a land packed full of surprises, and there had been many occasions when she had felt like a child in a toy-shop, running from one new discovery to the next only to find another waiting on the horizon.

It was an experience which she would not have wanted to miss, and she now admitted this freely to Max.

Kerry smiled to herself and shifted her position a little when her bottom began to object to the roughness of the fallen tree-trunk. Her glance shifted back to where Max was working on the vehicle, and her thoughts slipped their rein again to career off in a different direction.

As the country had unfolded before her, so had the nature of the man whom she had known first by his work. Max was intelligent and enlightened and he could be painfully direct, but he had a way with people that gained him their trust and their respect. He was by nature a caring and considerate man, but his warm and giving personality did not always come to the fore.

Kerry stared at Max's lean male hips encased in snug-fitting khaki shorts, and allowed her glance to stray freely down along those powerful legs to the canvas shoes on his feet.

He was also incredibly sexy.

Stop it, Kerry! she told herself. She fanned herself frantically, but that wave of heat surging through her had nothing to do with the climate. You've got a one-track mind lately, and you'd better control it!

Max lowered the bonnet of the Range Rover with a loud snap that startled two crows out of a nearby tree, and Kerry rose self-consciously to her feet.

'I think we can forget about spending the night in Windhoek,' he said, a frown creasing his glistening brow as he wiped his greasy hands on a cloth and glanced at his watch. 'The next best town is Usakos, but that's nearly two hundred kilometres away, and on these roads I doubt if we'll get there before eight this evening.'

Kerry could see her chances of a cleansing, relaxing bath flying off into the distance with the crows, and a grimace marred her delicate features as she brushed a stray strand of hair out of her face. If her hair looked as lifeless as it felt, then her general appearance must be rather pathetic, but there was some consolation for her in knowing that Max was not looking so good himself. His hair was spiking on to his forehead, and there were definite signs of dust and grime on the T-shirt he was pulling on to his sweaty body.

'Do we push on to Usakos?' he asked her.

Jogged out of her reflective mood, Kerry glanced at the gravel road which seemed to trail on into eternity, and gestured wearily with her hands. 'Unless we feel like spending another night in a tent, then I don't think we have a choice,' she shrugged.

'You're right. After three nights on an inflatable mattress I'm more than ready for something softer.' He opened the door on the passenger side and waved her in. 'We've wasted enough time, so let's get moving.'

Max was not far out with his calculations. It was eight-thirty that evening when they arrived in Usakos, and they were both tired and hungry and longing for a bath.

Kerry waited outside in the loaded Range Rover while Max went into the hotel to arrange accommodation and parking facilities, but when he returned some minutes later there was a look on his weary face that told her something was not as it ought to be.

'What's the problem?' she asked when he climbed in beside her and slammed the door shut.

'We'll have to share a room.'

She stared at his tired, rugged profile and swallowed convulsively to hold back her laughter. 'You can't be serious,' she croaked.

'Does it look as if I'm joking?' he demanded, turning on her angrily, and she shrank back against the door with a myriad thoughts racing through her mind. 'The place is fully booked, it's late, and we're in desperate need of a bath and a decent bed to sleep on.' His piercing, glowering glance held hers in the dim interior of the vehicle. 'Do you have any serious objection to sharing a room with me?'

Kerry could think of several, but her rumbling stomach and her tired, aching body warned her that this was not the most appropriate moment to voice her objections. 'In the circumstances I don't think I can afford to quibble about it,' she sighed.

There had to be worse things on earth than having to share a room with Max for one night, she tried to reason with herself, but at that moment she could not think of any.

She stayed in the hotel foyer with their overnight luggage while Max garaged the Range Rover. She felt nervous and jumpy, and it didn't help to know that the young man at Reception was eyeing her with a great deal of curiosity and interest. Was he aware that she was not married to Max?

He tried to strike up a conversation with her, but she remained cool and aloof, and she was actually relieved when she saw Max's tall, familiar figure striding into the foyer.

The young man snapped to attention when he saw Max. 'Will you be dining in the restaurant, sir, or shall I take your order now and have it sent up to your room?'

Kerry felt herself sagging mentally and physically at the thought of having to dress for dinner, and Max must have echoed that feeling.

'We'll order now,' he said without hesitation, glancing at Kerry. 'What will you have?'

'A nice thick steak with all the trimmings, and a decent pot of coffee,' she replied, her mouth watering as her mind conjured up a mental vision of what she had ordered.

'Make that two steaks,' Max requested the desk clerk, and the young man jotted down their order before signalling a uniformed man to show them to their room.

Kerry could not decide whether it was nerves or sheer tiredness that made her legs shake so much when they followed the hotel porter up the carpeted stairs. She *was* tired, but she was also extremely nervous, and there was no point in trying to deny it as the hotel porter unlocked the door to their room and carried their suitcases inside.

The first thing Kerry noticed was the king-sized bed, and she felt herself going hot and cold in rapid succession while Max tipped the porter, but she somehow made it across the room, and was standing in front of the open window when she heard the porter leave and close the door firmly behind him.

She could feel Max's eyes boring into her back, but waited until she felt certain she had regained control of herself before she turned to face him. 'Does the desk clerk know that we—that we're not——?'

'Your reputation is still intact,' Max interrupted with an unexpected harshness in his voice that made her wince inwardly. 'I signed us in as Mr and Mrs Harper. Satisfied?'

'Thank you.' She could feel herself blushing, but she did not look away. 'I suppose you think I'm being silly.'

His taut features relaxed a fraction, but not enough to soften the tightness about his mouth. 'I don't like this situation any better than you do, Kerry, and I shouldn't have to explain why.'

The expression in his eyes made her pulses quicken in response, and embarrassment was deepening the colour in her cheeks when he turned from her to stride into the bathroom.

She could hear him running water into the bath, and her face wore a pensive expression as she hoisted her suitcase on to the bed to take out what she would be needing for the night. She had to agree with Max—explanations were quite unnecessary. The emotions simmering directly beneath the surface of their business relationship would need very little encouragement to erupt into an inferno of desire, and getting herself into a state of panic was not going to help them through this awkward situation.

Max came up behind her, the carpeted floor and the sound of running water muting his footsteps. He touched her arm to get her attention, and she almost leapt out of her skin. So much for letting herself get into a panic! she thought cynically as she looked up to see Max gesturing towards the bathroom.

'You go first,' he said, but Kerry shook her head.

'I'd prefer it if you used the bathroom first,' she explained, fighting to control her heartbeat. 'I need to shampoo my hair, and I know I'm going to be in there for ages.'

'As you wish,' he agreed curtly, taking a few articles of clothing out of his suitcase and returning to the bathroom. The door closed behind him, the taps were turned off, and Kerry felt herself relaxing when she heard him splashing in the bath.

She was glad to be alone for a while to come to terms with the situation, and her glance swept the room for the first time, taking in the cool blue and white striped curtains and pale grey carpet. The built-in cupboards and dressing-table had a white enamelled finish, and so did the panelled headboard of the king-sized bed.

Kerry felt her throat constrict and her heart started to pound against her ribs with the force of those forbidden desires which were becoming so increasingly difficult to keep in check. How was she going to spend the long hours of the night on that enormous bed without—God help her—touching Max or wanting to be touched?

There was a certain element of fear attached to that tantalising thought as it careered through her mind, but her body had no conscience, and even as she stood there surveying the room she could feel the first stirrings of that hot, aching need inside her.

She drew a deep, audible breath in an attempt to steady herself. She had to hang on tightly to her resolve. In a few days this entire ordeal would be over. Max would be on his way to Australia, and then her own life would settle back into that comfortable routine of the past.

The sound of bathwater draining away reached her ears, and then the taps were turned on again. Kerry held her breath for no explicable reason, and expelled it again slowly when Max emerged from the bathroom with his discarded clothes bundled in his hands.

He was wearing clean black jogging shorts and a blue short-sleeved shirt which he had left unbuttoned down the front. His square, resolute jaw was clean-shaven, and his dark hair lay damp and tousled across his broad forehead. He also smelled nice, she was thinking as she passed him on her way to the bathroom he had vacated, and her irrational senses stirred in response to the now familiar scent of his shaving cream and cologne.

She washed her hair and wrapped a small towel around her head before she slid down into the hot bath. She allowed herself a couple of minutes to ease the tiredness and the tension out of her muscles, but her mind picked up her earlier thoughts and went on from there.

She was expecting her life to revert to what it had been before this trip, but she wondered about it now. Was it going to be so easy for her to settle back into that old, comfortable routine she had left behind to fulfil this assignment?

Uncertainty dug its claws into her. Why?

She tried to consider the situation rationally and calmly while she lay back in the bath, but somehow—no matter from what angle she looked at it—her future was beginning to appear bleak and empty without Max's presence to add that vital spark to her existence.

Kerry reached agitatedly for the soap to wash away the dust and sweat of four days on the road without a decent bath.

Why did she feel so depressed at the thought of never seeing Max again? She was not in love with him. She *couldn't* be, she reasoned with herself angrily. What she felt for him was purely physical. It was what Josie would call a delicious surge of lust. That was *all* it was—lust! And she ought to be ashamed of herself!

But Kerry was *not* ashamed of herself. Wanting Max and wanting to be with him had become synonymous, and it had taken hold of her so naturally that it felt as comfortable as breathing.

I couldn't be in love with him, could I? A goading little voice at the back of her mind started plying her with questions that made her squirm. Why did the sky seem to cloud over whenever he failed to greet her with a smile in the mornings? Why did she always listen for his voice and find such pleasure in its deep, velvety resonance? Why did she find his many little gestures of kindness and concern towards others—and towards herself—so endearing?

Kerry groaned inwardly and sank down into the bath, submerging her soapy body until the water lapped against her chin. She liked the man; she liked everything about him, but she could not be in love with him. She dared not even *think* of loving him! There would be no future in it for her, and it would be to her own advantage to remember that.

She shelved her thoughts forcibly and got out of the bath. She was tired and hungry, and for some obscure reason she was allowing her mind to drag the entire situation out of its proper perspective.

Max was sitting on one of the high-backed chairs with his long legs stretched out in front of him when Kerry came out of the bathroom, and his glance swept her briefly, almost impersonally, from the small towel which was still wound around her head down to her bare toes curling into the carpet.

'Are you hungry?' he asked, waving a hand towards the tray on the small square table between the chairs.

'I'm starving!' she groaned as she bundled her dirty clothes into her suitcase and joined him at the table.

They lifted the lids which had kept their food warm, and Kerry's insides were actually beginning to shake with hunger as she spread a serviette across her knees.

The steak was tender and succulent, the salads were fresh, and the potato chips had been fried just long enough to leave them soft beneath the crispy outer layer. It was perhaps not a meal one would recommend as a healthy daily diet, but Kerry could feel her insides snatching it up greedily after several days of having nothing but tinned food warmed up on a gas cooker.

She shivered at the sudden coolness of the breeze that entered the room, and she was still contemplating what to do about it when Max got up to close the window.

'Usakos lies close to the edge of the Namib desert, and it's about a hundred and fifty kilometres west of the sea,' he said when he resumed his seat at the small table. 'That's why the day temperatures are high while the nights are tempered by the sea breeze blowing inland.'

That explained the sudden drop in temperature, but her mind was occupied with a more pressing query that needed an answer. 'How long do we have in Windhoek before we fly back to Johannesburg?' she asked.

'Almost three days.' He observed her intently as he speared the last piece of tomato on his plate with his fork and popped it into his mouth. 'Are you looking forward to going home?'

'Ye-es.'

'You don't sound very sure,' he commented.

Kerry paused to consider this as she swallowed down her last mouthful of food and deposited her empty plate in the tray. 'I feel as if I'm being torn in two,' she confessed while she poured their coffee. 'I'm looking forward to going home, but I also regret having to leave Namibia.'

'All this rugged beauty can have an extraordinary effect on one,' said Max.

'It's like a drug,' she agreed, passing him his cup of coffee and settling back in her chair with her own. 'I've seen so much these past weeks, and yet I want to see more.'

'I feel the same way about it.'

She smiled. 'I'm glad you said that, because I was beginning to think I'm going crazy.'

There was no answering smile in the eyes that held hers. 'Perhaps we're both going a little crazy.'

'Perhaps you're right.'

Her heart started to flutter like a caged bird in her breast when Max's glance held hers captive. Why did she have this strange feeling that they were sharing an intimate knowledge rather than discussing their mixed feelings about leaving Namibia?

Don't be ridiculous! she rebuked herself sharply. She was letting her imagination run away with her again, and that would never do.

They finished their coffee, and Kerry rose from the table to towel her hair dry while Max deposited the tray in the passage outside their bedroom door.

'Which side of the bed do you prefer, Kerry?'

The unexpectedness of that question jolted her nerves and, using the towel as a shield to hide her embarrassment from him, she answered him in the same brisk tone. 'I'll take the left side.'

'Good choice.'

Kerry heard the laughter in his voice and felt the firm grip of his hands on her shoulders as he propelled her backwards. The edge of the bed caught her behind the knees and she sat down heavily.

'I think you're enjoying my discomfort,' she accused him sharply when he kneeled beside her on the bed and took over the task of drying her hair.

'It's such a rarity to find a woman of your age who still blushes that I can't somehow resist the temptation to tease you.' He stopped drying her hair suddenly, and the heat radiating from his body aroused the most disquieting sensations when he slid his fingers beneath her chin and tipped her face to the side so that she was forced to look at him. 'You see?' he announced triumphantly. 'You *are* blushing!'

His eyes teased and mocked her simultaneously, and Kerry cursed herself for not being more worldly as she felt that embarrassing warmth stinging her cheeks.

'This is a very awkward situation, Max,' she defended herself in a voice which was not quite steady.

'Pretend I'm your brother.'

She felt like laughing. There was nothing sisterly about the way her senses were responding to the clean male smell of him. 'I'm not very good at pretending,' she confessed.

'Neither am I.'

His eyes roamed the delicate contours of her face while he stroked the sensitive underside of her jaw with his thumb, and Kerry felt the breath lock in her throat when his glance lingered with dark intent on her soft, generous mouth.

'I didn't plan this, Kerry,' he told her.

'I know.' The atmosphere had become much too tense, and she injected a light, teasing note into her voice as she asked, 'Are you going to help me dry my hair, or aren't you?'

Max's hands fell away from her as his throaty laugh instantly eased the tension between them. 'Kneel in front of me,' he instructed, shifting his position to the centre of the enormous bed. 'It'll make it easier for me to dry your hair.'

Kerry did as she was told. She knelt in front of him on the bed with her knees fitting snugly between his, and steadying herself with her hands on his hard, muscular thighs was somehow the most natural thing to do while he rubbed her hair vigorously with the towel.

'I think that should do,' he announced some minutes later, his glance capturing hers when he discarded the towel, and Kerry swallowed nervously as he used his fingers to comb the slightly damp tendrils of hair away from her face.

The silence that settled between them was suddenly strained and heavily charged with suppressed emotions. Max's dark, smouldering eyes questioned Kerry's while his fingers trailed an exploratory, fiery path along the sensitive column of her slender neck, and her pent-up feelings escaped their tight rein despite all her efforts to the contrary.

Her conscience warned that she ought to put a stop to this situation while there was still time, but her throbbing pulses told her that it was already too late. She wanted him; she wanted him so badly that her body was aching for his touch, and there was no point in denying this to herself when her eyes must have given him the answer he had been seeking.

'I want you, Kerry,' he warned throatily. 'I want to hold you, and touch you, and do things to you that will please you as much as I know you will please me.'

'Don't... say that!' she protested weakly.

'But it's the truth.'

This was Kerry's cue to move away, to place a safe distance between Max and herself, but instead she remained where she was, mesmerised by what he was saying and her own physical response to it.

He lowered his head until she could feel his warm breath mingling with hers, and for one brief instant she was thinking rationally again. 'Please, Max, we—we've got to be sensible about this.'

'I know, but how can I be sensible about it while I'm convinced that you want me as much as I want you?' He cupped her face in his hands and his mouth teased hers into submission with tantalising, feather-light kisses until she dug her fingernails into his taut thighs and leaned into him with a need for more, but he backed away, his eyes probing hers. 'You do want me, don't you, Kerry?'

'Yes. Oh, yes, you—you know I do, but...' Her voice faltered into silence as his palms rested briefly against the side of her breasts before he untied the belt of her cotton robe and slid it off her shoulders.

'But what?' he demanded softly against her eager, quivering lips.

You still have time to save yourself! her conscience prodded her. Say something—quickly! Before it's too late!

Kerry could not ignore the advice her conscience had given her. 'Aren't you forgetting that we're supposed to stick to the rules of a business relationship?' she asked.

'Rules were made to be broken if all the concerned parties are in agreement,' he said, his fingers dipping beneath the narrow, lacy straps of her flimsy nightdress and lifting them off her smooth, creamy shoulders to pave the way for the sensual exploration of his mouth.

Shivers of pleasure raced along her receptive nerves, and Kerry felt herself tremble beneath Max's experienced hands when her nightdress slid down her body to leave her naked from the waist up. Her breasts were swelling to his gentle touch as he cupped them in his hands, and a shuddering sigh of delight escaped her when he raked his thumbs back and forth across their hardening peaks.

'Oh, Max, you—you remind me of the businessman who once told me that the secret of success lies in never entering into an agreement which doesn't have an escape hatch for—for emergencies.'

Her voice had sounded throaty and unfamiliar to her own ears. It hadn't been easy trying to speak while her body was becoming acquainted with a rush of heated sensations she had never experienced before.

'I'd say this is an emergency, wouldn't you, Kerry?'

This is an emergency all right! she was thinking a little frantically as he lowered his dark head over her left breast to tongue the nipple into an aching button. Oh, Josie, I wonder what you'd say if you could see me now and know what I'm thinking and feeling!

'I think all parties are in agreement that we—we use the escape hatch, and...' Her voice faded on a moan of pure ecstasy as Max took her taut, aching nipple into his warm, moist mouth and sucked it gently.

'And what?' he prompted, turning his attention to her other breast and tonguing the nipple which was already taut and puckered with desire.

'I hope we don't regret this,' she said, lacing her fingers through his hair to detain him when he drew away from her. 'Oh, Max, don't stop!'

He smiled. 'I don't intend to, my beautiful Kerry, but let's get rid of our clothes first.'

He drew her up off the bed so that her nightdress and her robe slid to the floor at her feet to leave her naked except for her lacy bikini panties. He released her for an instant to shrug himself out of his shirt and drop his shorts, then he caught her up against him as if he could no longer wait to feel her soft, womanly flesh against his.

The heat of his aroused body inflamed her, and the searing hunger of his kiss awakened her to a matching hunger that left them both dazed when they paused to draw breath.

He lowered her on to the bed, the abrasiveness of his chest hair against her nipples exciting her, and she drew his head down, inviting the intimate invasion of his mouth once again.

Max aroused her skilfully, leaving no room for doubt in her mind when he finally eased her panties down her thighs. She raised her knees slightly, making it easier for him, and then the final barrier between them was discarded.

Kerry was a trembling mass of exciting sensations. Every nerve and sinew in her heated body had come alive to his touch, and she was scarcely aware that she was breathing when his fingers trailed a tantalising caress along the soft inner flesh of her quivering thighs.

Touch me! Please touch me, Max! she begged him silently while her hands made their own eager exploration of his muscular frame.

His mouth shifted over hers as if he had heard her silent request, his kisses draining her mind of coherent thought and stifling her soft wail of pleasure when his fingers finally probed the intimate core of her womanhood. He stroked her gently and rhythmically, piling sensation upon sensation until she was mindless to everything except the near-frantic desire to assuage that exquisite, aching need inside her.

Kerry had gone beyond the point where she might have wanted to question the wiseness of her actions. Her hips were arching towards Max of their own volition and making jerky, thrusting little movements which she could not control as her excitement mounted to a near-intolerable peak. She wanted to be closer to him, she wanted him inside her with a need far greater than she had ever known before, and it must have been instinct, rather than knowledge, that guided her hand when she reached the stage where she felt she could no longer bear this sweet torture.

Her touch drew a shuddering groan of pleasure from Max, and it was with an almost savage urgency that he parted her thighs with his knees prior to entering her in one long, hard thrust.

Kerry had drawn an audible breath at the unexpected stab of discomfort his penetration had aroused, but in that moment of passionate urgency the incident had gone unnoticed, and a feeling of relief swamped her.

He didn't know! He didn't suspect! And she wasn't going to tell him!

This felt so right, she was thinking. She belonged to Max; they belonged together, but reality sneaked into this perfect moment and brought with it an unwanted stab of fear when she realised that Max was holding her without moving or speaking. Had she been mistaken? Did he suspect, after all?

'Please, Max! Please!' she begged hoarsely, her cheeks flushed and her eyes stormy with the emotions he had aroused. 'Make love to me! Please don't stop!'

'Oh, God!' he growled throatily, his dark eyes glazed with the extent of his desire as she wound her legs about his taut thighs. 'I couldn't stop now even if I wanted to!'

He thrust himself into her again and again, raising her each time to new heights of pleasure until that exquisite, aching tension snapped inside her and suffused her body with a glowing satisfaction which was in itself so intense that it brought tears to her eyes.

Max sagged on top of her, his throbbing release coming seconds after her own, and she cushioned his sweat-dampened body, holding him to her with her legs and her arms until their laboured breathing subsided and their heartbeats slowed.

If only she could hold him to her like this forever. If only...!

Reality was like an icy hand curling its fingers about her heart, squeezing it painfully. She could not hold Max. There were no chains with which to bind him to her, and neither did she want that. Her mother had told her once, If you love something, set it free.

Love?

The word caught her on the raw. This was the worst possible moment to discover the true depth of her feelings. Her throat tightened achingly on tears she dared not shed, and when Max eventually withdrew from her she let him go without attempting to hold him back.

He sat on the edge of the bed with his back turned towards her, his elbows resting on his knees and his head in his hands.

Kerry sat up cautiously and dragged the sheet about her naked body. They had been so intimately close a moment ago, and she wanted to reach out, to touch him, but she was suddenly afraid to.

What was he thinking? Had she perhaps done something wrong?

'Max?' His name came out on a croak and she cleared her throat nervously. 'What's the matter?'

He dropped his hands and left them hanging between his knees, but his eyes remained on the carpet. 'We were in agreement about wanting each other, weren't we?'

'Yes, of course.' She held her breath.

'Then why do I feel like a cad?' He turned at last to pin her down with troubled eyes. 'Tell me!' he insisted, brushing an agitated hand over the back of his tousled head. 'Why do I feel as if I took something that didn't belong to me?'

Stay calm, Kerry! she told herself.

'You took only what I was willing to give, and in return you've given me a memory I shall cherish for the rest of my life,' she answered him quietly.

'Is that supposed to make me feel better?' he demanded on a harsh laugh.

'It should,' she said, her heart thudding nervously in her breast as she reached down to the floor for her nightdress, but his hand was there before hers, and the flimsy garment was flung beyond her reach.

'You won't need that,' he growled, getting back into bed and pulling her down into his arms. 'I'm going to make love to you again before this night is over, and I'm damned if I'm going to feel guilty about it!'

Kerry didn't say anything. She couldn't. His mouth had taken possession of hers, and her body was already responding to the magical caress of his hands.

She had no regrets.

CHAPTER EIGHT

KERRY stood with her eyes closed in the shower cubicle while a therapeutic jet of steaming water pummelled her body. It was ironic. Three weeks ago she had wished herself back in Windhoek, but now that she was here she wished she could have these past weeks over again.

She had lain awake for most of the night, listening to Max's deep, even breathing and savouring every moment of his nearness as if it were a precious jewel. In the sober light of day they had avoided each other's eyes, and during the drive from Usakos to Windhoek they had spoken only when it had been absolutely necessary. What had happened between them was best forgotten, but Kerry had known that it occupied Max's thoughts as much as her own.

Exhaustion had sent her up to her room after lunch, and she had slept for several hours that afternoon while Max returned the Range Rover to the company from whom he had hired it. She had got up at five to take a shower before changing for dinner, and now she was thinking, What if...?

Most of her thoughts were suddenly beginning with the words what if...? What if she could persuade Max to take her with him on his travels? What if she told him that she would agree to an intimate working relationship with no strings attached?

Kerry shook herself mentally and turned the taps to shut off the jet of water. She was thinking with her heart, not her head, and in the process she was losing her sense of direction. She might have overstepped the mark last night, but that did not mean she was ready to cast aside everything she had always believed in.

She shook her glossy fair hair free of the shower cap before stepping out of the cubicle, and was towelling herself dry when she became aware of the fact that there was a man standing in the bathroom doorway. Shock made her breath lock painfully in her throat and she was blinded for an instant to the fact that it was Max, but recognition did not prevent her face from flaming with embarrassment.

'How did you get in?' she demanded weakly, holding her towel against her for protection and leaning back against the shower cubicle's sliding glass door while the lameness of relief poured into her legs.

'Your bedroom door was unlocked, and when you didn't hear me knock . . .' He left his sentence unfinished and gestured expressively with one strong, sun-browned hand.

'What do you want?' she asked, thinking how silly it was that she could still feel embarrassed about appearing naked before him after the intimacy they had shared the night before.

'I found this in the Range Rover,' he said, holding up a small bottle of shampoo for her inspection.

Her pulses fluttered with an awareness which her mind refused to acknowledge. 'It must have fallen out of my bag.'

His glance flicked over her and desire sparked in his dark eyes. Kerry's mind registered that look at last, and her treacherous body warmed and tingled in response as if he had actually touched her.

Don't do this to me, Max, she thought. Don't make me want you. This time I might not want to let you go again.

The atmosphere was tense and strained. Were his thoughts perhaps similar to her own? She could not tell, and neither did she have time to dwell on it.

The bottle of shampoo was flung on to a chair, and one long stride was all Max needed to reach her. He caught her up against him, his hands against her back burning her skin, and her strangled protest died on her lips when his hard mouth closed over hers with a hunger that demanded and found an equally fierce response in her.

Kerry was being propelled towards that emotional edge of not caring about anything except the urgent need to assuage that insatiable longing inside her, and she could already feel herself yielding to it when Max eased his mouth from hers to seek out that sensitive little hollow behind her ear.

'You always smell so nice,' he murmured throatily. 'That's something I'll always remember about you.'

'You sound as if you're saying goodbye,' she managed in a breathy voice, holding the towel in position with one hand and wedging the other between them. 'Are you saying goodbye?'

'I believe I am,' he said, his arms falling away from her to leave her cold and trembling.

'How much time do you need to say goodbye?' She tried to laugh off the dreaded implication of his words.

Max didn't answer her. He merely looked at her for a long time with an unfathomable expression in his eyes, and she was beginning to feel awkward and uncomfortable when he turned away to pick up the cotton robe she had left draped across the seat of the toilet.

'Put this on,' he said, holding the robe for her to slip her arms into the sleeves. 'You're much too alluring with just a towel draped in front of you.'

'Thank you,' she murmured shakily, standing with her back to him while she fastened the belt about her waist with unsteady fingers.

'There's been a change of plan,' he told her.

She turned and looked up at him with eyes that failed to conceal that feeling of dread inside her. 'What do you mean?' she asked.

'I received a message from my contact in Australia. He's managed to round up a camera crew and they'll be ready to start shooting the documentary the day after tomorrow.'

Kerry's face paled and it felt as if a piece of lead had suddenly lodged itself in her chest. She had known that this moment would come, and she had prepared herself for it, but...so soon?

'Does this mean you have to leave immediately?' she asked, holding her breath.

'Yes.'

'That's rather short notice, isn't it?'

'It is, but I managed to get the only available seat on this evening's flight out to Johannesburg, and I leave for Perth in the morning.' Max's gaze rested for a moment on the hand she had lifted to her aching throat, and his mouth tightened. 'There's no need for you to change your travel plans, but if you'd prefer to hasten your departure then the desk clerk will make the necessary flight arrangements for you.'

Kerry was beginning to feel claustrophobic in the confined space of the bathroom and she brushed past Max to enter the bedroom. He followed her, and she could feel his eyes resting on her back as she walked barefoot across the carpeted floor to stand at the window.

'How long will you be staying in Australia?' she asked, staring blindly out across the city.

'Six months—perhaps longer. I can't be sure.'

Her mouth suddenly felt as dry as the Namib desert. Fool! Idiot! Six months; a year; an eternity. What did it matter how long he would be away? They had spent almost every waking moment of the past three weeks together, and they had shared one brief night of intimacy. She had known from the beginning that Max would have nothing more to offer her, and if she was hurting now she had only herself to blame for it.

She moistened her dry lips with the tip of her tongue and swallowed convulsively at the tightness in her throat, but her face was rigidly controlled when she turned her back on the window to confront Max. 'What time does your flight leave?' she asked.

'Eight-thirty,' he said, taking his hand out of the pocket of his khaki trousers to glance at his watch.

Take me with you, Max! she begged silently.

He looked away, his jaw hardening as if he had heard her, and Kerry felt the sting of his rejection even though the words had not gone beyond a wailing plea in her mind.

'I still have some packing to do, but I'll see you before I leave,' he said curtly, and moments later she was alone in her room.

Kerry drew a choking breath and sat down heavily on the padded stool in front of the dressing-table. She had been looking forward to spending these last few days in Windhoek with Max before they went their separate ways, but everything was suddenly moving much too fast towards that dreaded moment of parting.

Perhaps it was all working out for the best, she tried to reason with herself. Lingering farewells were always doubly painful, but—oh, God—why did it have to be so soon?

Kerry pinned her hair up into a neat chignon and donned the blue dress she had worn that first night in Windhoek three weeks ago. A light application of blusher hid the paleness in her cheeks, but there was nothing she could do to disguise the haunted look in her eyes that changed their colour from clear blue to deep violet.

'Oh, Max! Max!' She wasn't conscious of the fact that she whispered her thoughts out loud while she replaced the cap of her coral-pink lipstick. 'If only you could have loved me a little! If you'd loved me then we could have worked something out.'

She picked up her watch and strapped it to her slender wrist. It was a quarter to seven. Max would have to leave for the airport soon. She stood up and examined herself closely in the mirror. She looked calm and serene, but in actual fact she felt blessedly numb. The feelings were all there, bottled up tightly inside her, but not for anything in the world was she going to let him see what a complete idiot she had been.

The sharp knock on her bedroom door was expected, since Max had said he would see her before he left, but still it jolted her insides and clutched painfully at her throat.

This is it! she told herself.

She opened the door and they stared at each other in silence for seemingly endless seconds before she stood aside for Max to enter. She registered the fact that he was wearing his lightweight beige suit and blue open-necked shirt, but her attention was caught and held by that tiny nerve tugging at the corner of his tight mouth.

What did it mean? she wondered, giving the door a gentle push until it clicked shut.

'You look lovely, Kerry,' he said with an odd note in his voice while he surveyed her with those deceptively lazy eyes. 'I wish we could have dined together this evening.'

That tightness in her chest was making it almost too painful to breathe. If she didn't do something quickly she was going to humiliate herself by bursting into tears.

'Where do you want me to send the photographs and slides once they've been processed?' she asked in what she hoped was her best professional manner.

'I'd appreciate it if you could deliver them to my sister's home in Houghton,' he said, drawing the curtain aside at the window to stare down into the well-lit street below. 'Kathleen will keep them safe for me until I get back. Will you see to that?'

'Yes, of course.' Her throat was aching with tears she dared not shed, and the slow, painful thudding of her heart seemed to fill the silent room while she fought to regain control of her vocal cords. 'I'm glad I had the opportunity to share a little of your working life with you. Now I'll appreciate your books that much more.'

He dropped the curtain back into place with an angry gesture, and she was almost unnerved by the probing intensity of his glance when he turned to face her.

'Do you have any regrets, Kerry?' he demanded.

She knew that he was not referring to the business side of their brief relationship, and she could feel that hateful warmth stealing into her cheeks, but her glance did not waver from his when she said, 'No, not one.'

She was subjected to a long, hard stare, and she was once again aware of that nerve jumping at the corner of his mouth.

He looked as if he was caught in the middle of an emotional crisis. Was it possible that he disliked the idea of having to leave her? Would he perhaps change his mind and take her with him? Don't be ridiculous! she admonished herself sharply, crushing that flicker of hope in her heart while it was still in its infancy.

'It's also been a privilege for me to know you, and to work with you, Kerry,' he said into the silence that had once again settled between them.

'If we're not careful this is going to develop into a mutual admiration society!' She had tried to brush off his remark as a joke, but her smile had gone awry, and her lips were quivering with suppressed tears.

'I wish we had more time, but I have to go,' Max said quietly.

'I know.'

Kerry swallowed convulsively on that tightness in her throat. She wanted to touch him; she wanted to feel his arms around her just once more before he walked away from her, but she knew it would only prolong the agony.

He reached out to touch her, but his fingers were inches away from her face when he halted the action and let his hand fall to his side again. 'Goodbye, Kerry.'

She winced inwardly at the flat finality in his voice. Not goodbye, Max! she wanted to say. Don't say goodbye as if we're never going to see each other again! Those words were never spoken. They remained locked in her heart as Max turned his back on her, and stinging tears blurred her vision as the door clicked shut behind him.

It was Sunday, and Kerry was thinking, Tomorrow will be the start of a new week and a new beginning for me.

If she looked out through the kitchen window she could see the setting sun tint the sky a delicate pink, but she turned her back on it resolutely. It made her recall all those spectacular sunsets she had watched with Max, and she couldn't think of it yet without wanting to cry.

She had arrived back in Johannesburg on the same day Max had been due to leave for Australia, and for five days she had seen no one and had spoken to no one except Calvin MacCullum. He had telephoned on the off-chance that she would be back to offer her an assignment, but she had turned it down.

Three days ago she had not been ready to do anything constructive with her life while her mood had still fluctuated between fits of 'I'm feeling sorry for myself' tears and bouts of helpless 'Why did it have to happen to me?' rage.

She realised now that if she wanted to regain her emotional stability she would have to work. She would have to keep herself busy, *very* busy, and in time she might begin to forget that she had given her love where it had not been wanted.

The chime of the doorbell startled her out of her reverie. Only Calvin MacCullum knew that she was back, but he never called on her socially. The doorbell chimed with a little more urgency the second time, and Kerry finally managed to set her limbs in motion.

She opened the door, and a furious Josie stormed past her into the house with eyes that sparked green fire.

'Why did I have to hear via the grapevine that you were back in Johannesburg?' she demanded sharply. 'Why didn't you call me?'

'I've been busy.' Busy weeping and wailing, and wallowing in my own misery, Kerry added silently in a ruthless attempt to mock her pathetic behaviour during the past few days.

'Too busy to call an old friend who happens to care about you?' Josie rapped back, and Kerry had to admit defeat.

'I've brewed a fresh pot of filter coffee,' she said by way of an apology. 'Would you like to join me?'

Josie mellowed down to a near-smile. 'I'd love a cup of your coffee.'

Kerry led the way into the kitchen and switched on the light before she drew the curtains across the window to shut out the fading pink glow of sunset in the darkening sky. Sunsets would always make her think of Max, but she did not want to think about him now.

'Well?' Josie prompted inquisitively as they sat facing each other across the kitchen table with a steaming cup of aromatic coffee in front of them.

'Well what?' Kerry echoed evasively, hugging her misery to her bosom like a selfish child who refused to relinquish a favourite toy to a friend.

'I want to know about your trip,' Josie elaborated impatiently.

'Namibia's a fascinating country.'

Josie was bristling with a mixture of annoyance and curiosity as she leaned forward in her chair and rested her elbows on the table. 'Is that all you're going to say?'

'I'll show you the photographs when they're ready.'

'Thanks!' Josie snorted disparagingly.

Kerry lapsed into a guilty silence.

'Hey, come on, Kerry! I'm your friend, remember?' Josie coaxed her quietly when she sensed that something was wrong. 'I'm the one you've always trusted enough to confide in. Why can't you trust me now?'

'It's not that I don't trust you, Josie, but I——' Kerry looked down at her cup and watched the light dancing in her coffee, but Max's face materialised before her eyes.

She pressed her fingers against her closed eyelids to shut out that image, but it remained etched on her mind. 'This goes deep,' she said thickly, swallowing at that nagging lump in her throat. 'It's almost too deep to talk about right now.'

Josie was silent for a long time before she asked, 'Did I have reason to chew my fingernails to the quick while you were away?'

'I did a very silly thing,' Kerry finally confessed on a tired sigh. 'I fell in love with Maxwell Harper.'

'Oh, lord!' Josie's cup went down into her saucer with a clatter. 'Does he know how you feel?'

'I didn't tell him, if that's what you mean, but he's not stupid, and I'm afraid he might have guessed.'

'You don't think there's a possibility he might feel the same way about you?'

'No, I don't.' Kerry laughed for the first time in days, but it was a laugh filled with all the raw, aching bitterness inside her. 'You know as well as I do that when a man finds a woman sexually attractive it doesn't necessarily follow that he should love her.'

Josie looked away as if she could not bear to see the naked pain in Kerry's eyes. 'Are you going to see him again?' she asked.

'I doubt it.' Kerry bit down hard on her quivering lip. 'Max has been in Australia for a week, and he'll be stationed there for the next six months or more.'

'What's to stop you from joining him there?' queried Josie.

'I couldn't go unless I'm invited, and he wouldn't do that, so there's no point in pursuing the relationship.'

'Are you just going to sit back and let this man slip away from you?' Josie demanded incredulously.

'I don't have a choice.' Kerry stared dismally down into her coffee. 'He made it very clear that marriage wouldn't blend well with his nomadic existence.'

'I would have thought that your profession as a photographer would have blended very well with his.'

A humourless smile curved Kerry's soft mouth. 'I thought so too, but it would have been a debatable point only if he'd returned my feelings.'

'If there's the slightest chance that he might care for you, then he could be made to change his mind, you know,' Josie persisted, but Kerry shook her head adamantly.

'I don't want to make him do anything he doesn't want to, Josie. If Max should change his mind, then it must be *his* decision, not mine.'

Kerry sipped her coffee and had to admit that she felt better now that she had told Josie everything. No, that was untrue. She had not told Josie everything. She could never tell her how totally careless and wanton she had been that night in Usakos.

Oh, Max! she groaned his name inwardly. Do you lie awake at night, wanting me as much as I want you, or have you already forgotten?

Her eyes filled with hot tears. She tried to blink them back, but they escaped on to her lashes and rolled down her cheeks before she could check them. She dashed them away angrily with the back of her hand, and pulled herself together, but when she looked up she saw Josie observing her with a rueful expression on her face.

'I'm sorry, Kerry. I feel that this is really all my fault.'

'No, it isn't.' Kerry somehow managed to control the second volley of tears before they spilled on to her cheeks. 'I walked into this situation with my eyes wide open. I knew that this could happen and, when it did, I made no attempt to stop it.'

'This isn't just a heavy crush. You really do love Maxwell Harper.' Josie said this as if she was grasping the gravity of the situation for the first time. 'You actually love this man enough to let him walk out of your life without lifting a finger to stop him.'

Long after Josie had gone Kerry was still thinking about what she had said, and it triggered a memory which had touched her vaguely that night in Usakos. Her mother had said something to her once which had had no meaning to her as a child, but now, as it all came back to her, she could understand what her mother had been trying to convey to her.

If you love something, set it free. If it comes back, it's yours. If it doesn't, it never was.

She wanted Max to come back into her life, she prayed that he would, but if he didn't then she would have to accept the fact that it was never meant to be.

Kerry parked her Peugeot station-wagon in the curved gravel driveway of the Stafford mansion in Houghton and checked her appearance briefly in the rear-view mirror before she got out and walked towards the imposing pillared entrance of the house.

She was wearing a little more make-up than usual for this meeting with Kathleen Stafford, but there had been nothing she could do to disguise the shadows which were now a permanent fixture beneath her eyes.

'You work too hard and you don't get enough sleep,' Josie had reprimanded her a few days ago when they had had lunch together in the city, and Kerry had not denied it.

Work had been her only salvation during these past two months. It was not a cure, but it did help, and adding another six, often eight hours to her normal working day was preferable to lying awake in her bed at night with nothing but her tormented thoughts for company.

A wry, faintly cynical smile curved Kerry's generous mouth as she walked up the shallow marble steps and rang the bell. The long hours might be physically wearying, she was thinking, but financially it was worth the effort.

A uniformed maid admitted her and gestured politely towards one of several doors leading off the tiled entrance hall. 'Mrs Stafford is expecting you, madam, and she's waiting for you in the library.'

Kathleen Stafford rose from her chair beside a tall Grecian urn when Kerry entered the room. 'I'm so glad you're punctual,' she said, gesturing towards the tray on the low table close to the chair she had vacated. 'The tea's freshly made and ready to be poured.'

Her warm, embracing smile reminded Kerry so much of Max that it wrenched painfully at her insides to cut off the polite response she had formulated in her mind, and it took a moment before she was calm enough to say, 'Max asked me to leave this package with you, Mrs Stafford.'

'Oh, yes, the photographs. I'd love to take a peek at them, but Max left strict instructions that I was not to touch them until he'd taken a look at them himself, and heaven only knows when that will be.' Kathleen divulged this information conversationally while she took the package from Kerry and locked it away in one of the drawers of the large mahogany desk. 'I hope Max didn't subject you to a lot of rough outdoor living while you were in Namibia?'

'I enjoy roughing it in the country whenever I get the chance,' Kerry confessed with pain darkening her eyes as she recalled those nights under the starry Namibian skies with Max.

'You and Max are two of a kind, then.' Kathleen was smiling when she straightened from her task and stepped round the desk. 'You must have worked well together.'

'We did.'

'Please sit down.' She waved Kerry into a chair and seated herself to pour their tea into those delicate rose-patterned porcelain cups which Kerry had admired from the moment she had entered the library. 'Do you take milk and sugar, Kerry?'

She used Kerry's name with an easy familiarity which was startling as well as pleasing. 'I take milk, but no sugar, thank you.'

'I hope you'll forgive me for saying so, but I'm convinced you've lost weight since the last time I saw you.' There was concern in Kathleen's assessing glance when she passed Kerry her cup of tea. 'Have you been ill recently?'

Kerry brushed aside her query with a careless, 'I've been rather busy lately.'

Kathleen did not pursue the matter. 'I spend most of my free time in this room,' she explained when she saw Kerry's nervous glance shift to the book-lined walls. 'I enjoy reading, and this is an adaptable room. It's always warm and cosy in the winter, but cool and airy in the summer.'

Kerry saw something in those grey-green eyes that made her suspect that Max's sister was lonely. 'Do you live alone, Mrs Stafford?' she asked.

'Please call me Kathleen,' she corrected hastily. 'Yes, I do live alone, and I admit that this is rather a large house for one person to be living in, but I simply don't have the courage to sell it, and...' A reminiscent look entered her eyes. 'There are so many memories locked up in this old house, and it would be an emotional wrench to part with it.'

'What about your daughter and son-in-law? Wouldn't they consider moving in here with you?'

'I've thought of that, but I know what it's like when you're young and newly married. You want to have your own home in which to build your own memories.'

'I suppose you're right,' Kerry conceded with a sadness brought on by a longing for something she knew she would never have.

Kathleen Stafford was an unaffected and easy person to talk to, and they sat talking for a long time in the library with the afternoon sun streaming into the room before Kerry noticed a framed photograph of Max on the low teak cupboard against the wall between the two tall windows. He was much younger then. And leaner. And his handsome features were still untouched by the harshness of life on the political front.

'That photograph of Max was taken shortly before his departure for England, and I think he was twenty-three at the time.' Kathleen proffered this information after following the direction of Kerry's gaze. 'He was a vital and very intense young man. I think he believed he could change the world with his forthright journalistic observations, but he learned about failure the hard way, and he still carries those scars today.'

Kerry absorbed this information like a thirsty sponge while she looked into Max's dark, smiling eyes, but she was prevented from passing comment as a tight ball of pain lodged itself at the centre of her chest.

'I can understand why Max has such a high regard for your work, Kerry.' Kathleen kept the conversation going and seemed not to notice Kerry's discomfort. 'The photographs you took of Mary-Joe's wedding are all so beautiful that they're having difficulty trying to decide which of them they'd like to have enlarged for their wedding album.'

Kerry wrenched her eyes away from that photograph on the teak table and made a concerted effort to pull herself together, but her mouth felt dry with nervousness and longing. 'Have you heard from Max?' she could not help asking.

'I've received three telephone calls from Australia during the two months he's been away, and that's quite unusual for Max, but the last time he called he said I wouldn't be hearing from him again for quite a while because he was going into a telephonically inaccessible part of the country.' Kathleen smiled at Kerry and gestured towards the tea-tray. 'Shall I order a fresh pot of tea?'

'Not for me, thank you.' Kerry rose quickly to her feet. 'I never intended to stay this long, and I really must be going.'

Kathleen nodded and rose as well to accompany her out of the house. 'I'm glad I've had this opportunity to get to know you, Kerry. I've enjoyed your company, and I hope I'm going to see you again soon,' she said.

No, not soon, Kathleen, Kerry was thinking when she turned her station-wagon round and headed down the driveway. She liked Kathleen Stafford, but being with her made it difficult not to think of Max, and she could not think of him as yet without pain and longing tearing away at her insides.

CHAPTER NINE

'FOUR *months*!' Kerry's usually calm voice was shrill with an anger born of despair. 'You'd think that after four months I'd have the sense to say, "To hell with Maxwell Harper," so that I can get on with my life as I did before!'

Josie cast a quick and embarrassed glance about the restaurant before she pinned Kerry down with a disapproving look in her green eyes. 'You're shouting, Kerry, and people are staring,' she muttered.

'I don't care if people are staring!' Kerry's angry glance held Josie's for an instant across the table, then she put down her knife and fork and pressed her fingers briefly against her throbbing temples. 'I think I'm going insane!' she groaned.

'You've been working much too hard,' Josie countered with a rebuke in her voice. 'What you need is a nice long holiday.'

'I've got to keep myself busy,' Kerry protested. 'I know I'll go crazy if I have to sit around all day long with nothing to do.'

'But you're going to kill yourself if you don't start putting on the brakes a little,' Josie warned concernedly, then a speculative look entered her eyes. 'You've been seeing quite a lot of Kathleen Stafford lately. Has she been giving you news of Max?'

'She seldom mentions him, and I don't want to ask.'

'Are you afraid she might guess how you feel about her brother?'

'I don't want to talk about it,' Kerry said stiffly, spearing her salad with her fork once again without bringing anything to her mouth.

Josie lapsed into a grim silence before she signalled to the waitress to remove their plates, and they were sitting drinking their coffee when she said, 'I have some news for you which might take your mind off Max for a while.'

'What news?' Kerry demanded warily.

'Your father's here in Johannesburg.'

The murmur of voices in the crowded restaurant seemed to rise to a crescendo, and Kerry almost choked on a mouthful of coffee. 'My *father*?' she echoed, not quite sure that she ought to believe Josie. 'Did you say my father's here in Johannesburg?'

Josie nodded soberly. 'He arrived this morning, and he'd like to meet you, but he said something about not being sure how you'd feel about it after he'd been unkind enough to slam the door in your face five years ago.' She eyed Kerry with a certain amount of curiosity. 'Do you know what he meant by that?'

'Yes.' Kerry's mouth tightened and her blue eyes darkened with remembered pain and disappointment. 'I made contact with my father through an agency five years ago, but he refused to have anything to do with me.'

Josie looked crushed. 'You never told me you'd tried to contact your father.'

Kerry lowered her gaze guiltily. She had told Max, but she had never thought to confide in Josie. Why had she told Max things about herself which she had not even told her best friend?

'It was too painful at that time to talk about it, and afterwards I just didn't consider it important enough to mention,' she explained, trying to smooth over the situation, and then a puzzling thought occurred to her. 'Why would my father have contacted you, Josie? How did he know we were friends?'

'Someone—he wouldn't mention who—had given him my name and had suggested that he use me as a go-between.'

It could only be someone from the agency, Kerry was thinking. Her father must have remembered the name of the agency through which she had contacted him, and they could have given him the names of several people who might have suggested that he contact her through Josie.

'Will you see him?' Josie asked, cutting in on her thoughts.

'I don't know, Josie. I really don't know.'

Why should she? Kerry asked herself. Her father had not wanted to see her five years ago, so why should she agree to meet him now? If meeting her would have raked up memories of a marriage he would rather forget, then why would he want to rake up those memories now?

'He's staying at the Sandton Sun.' Josie proffered the information matter-of-factly while she sipped at her coffee. 'If you should decide to meet him, then you'll find him in the Cavana Lounge at seven this evening, and he'll be wearing a red carnation.'

A red carnation! Bitterness tinged the smile that curved Kerry's mouth. Just imagine! Her father had to wear a red carnation so that she would be able to recognise him! How absolutely hilarious! How terribly sad!

'My mother used to love red carnations,' she said, her face pinched and a little pale. 'I wonder if my father still remembers that?'

'Why don't you meet him and ask him?'

Kerry looked up and smiled tritely. 'I might just do that.'

Kerry had been at war with herself for the remainder of that afternoon. She could not decide what she ought to do, but curiosity finally won the battle for her, and it was exactly seven o'clock that evening when she entered the Sandton Sun's Cavana Lounge.

Her searching glance swept the room and its occupants before settling on a man seated in a nook to her left. He was staring at her, his mouth gaping slightly as his gaze shifted from her fair hair down to the shimmering black dress hugging her slender, almost too thin body, and her heart leapt nervously in her breast.

This was her father. But he was a stranger. How should she behave? How would her mother have wanted her to behave?

Kerry squared her shoulders and walked towards him, her black high-heeled shoes sinking deep into the plush green carpet. 'You're wearing a red carnation, so you must be Edward Nelson?' He did not respond immediately, and she felt a stab of doubt. 'You *are* Edward Nelson, aren't you?'

'Yes, I am. Forgive me.' He had risen quickly and awkwardly, his blue gaze holding hers and one hand clutching at the back of the padded seat as if he needed support. 'If I seemed rude, then it's because the resemblance to your mother is so striking.'

He was slightly taller than Kerry, stocky in build, but muscled rather than plump. His hair might have been a light auburn in his youth, she was thinking, but now it was flecked liberally with grey.

Edward Nelson seemed to regain his composure as he waved Kerry in to the curved seat so that she sat facing him, and she studied him as intently as he was studying her, noting the pleasing symmetry of the angular features with the deep grooves running from his nose to his mouth. He must have been good-looking when he was younger, she decided, then she hardened herself against the thought.

'My mother died eight years ago,' she announced almost accusingly, and his eyes flickered as if she had stung him.

'I know.'

He said that so calmly that Kerry felt like taking him by the lapels of his expensively tailored jacket and shaking him until he felt some of the pain she had suffered after her mother's death.

'Who told you?' she demanded with a sharpness in her voice that would have betrayed her feelings if he had known her better.

'Let me get you something to drink and then we can talk,' he brushed aside her query to signal the waiter. 'What will you have?'

Kerry did not want a drink; she wanted to talk and get it over with! She had acquired an unnatural temper since her return from Namibia, but she managed to control it in this instance. 'I'll have a medium-dry sherry, thank you.'

Neither of them spoke while they waited for their drinks. They had begun to circle each other mentally like two opponents in an arena, assessing each other's strengths and weaknesses before launching an attack. The tension snapped between them when the waiter returned to their table, and they sipped quickly at their drinks as if they both needed reviving.

It was Edward Nelson who broke the prolonged silence between them. 'It was very unkind of me to turn you away five years ago when you tried to contact me, and I apologise for that.'

He spoke with a slight twang acquired after years of living in Australia, but Kerry was not thinking about his accent when she asked curtly, 'What made you change your mind?'

'My conscience has pricked me for a long time, but the crunch came when I met a straight-talking chap by the name of Maxwell Harper.'

'*Max*!' That familiar name exploded from her lips in something close to shock. Her face had paled beneath her carefully applied make-up and her hands were suddenly shaking so much that she had to put down her glass before she spilled the amber liquid on to her dress. 'You saw *Max*?'

'He stormed into my office three weeks ago, told me exactly what kind of stinker he thought I was, and shifted my conscience into gear by making me realise how much I'd hurt you by not wanting to acknowledge your existence.' Edward smiled wryly down into his whisky, and Kerry recognised something of herself in the way his mouth lifted slightly at the corners. 'It shook me, but I must admit I liked his style.'

'Max did that?' she queried dazedly, wondering what had prompted him to confront her father.

It surprised her that he had remembered what she had told him, and it astonished her even more to know that he had actually gone out of his way to bring about something which she had written off as impossible a long time ago.

'I'm happy to know you have a friend like Maxwell Harper who really cares about you, Kerry,' he told her.

Kerry could have corrected that statement, but she decided to let it pass as she reached for her glass to take a steadying sip of sherry. 'Why did you turn me away five years ago?' she asked him.

'Shock initially, and then fear.'

'Fear?' she echoed in surprise, and her father looked at her with a sunny, twisted smile hovering about his mouth.

'I was afraid that meeting you after all these years would stir up old and painful memories.'

'Painful?' she echoed again in bewilderment. 'Do you find the memory of your marriage to my mother painful?'

'Yes, I do.' He held her glance for an instant, then infuriated her once again by changing the subject at a vital point in their conversation. 'Have you had dinner, Kerry?'

'No,' she almost snapped at him.

'Neither have I.' He got up and held out his hand invitingly. 'Would you have dinner with me?'

'I'd like that, thank you,' she was surprised to hear herself saying as she rose to her feet and placed her hand in his for the first time to let him escort her from the Cavana Lounge to one of the hotel's restaurants.

Kerry studied the elaborate menu and asked for a small portion of fish with a salad, while her father opted for their steak speciality. She was still sipping the dry sherry she had brought with her from the lounge, but her father had finished his whisky and ordered himself another.

Edward Nelson kept the conversation going throughout dinner, questioning Kerry about her profession and touching on mundane subjects. He seemed determined not to enter into a serious discussion until after they had eaten, and Kerry had to concede a temporary defeat.

A strained silence settled between them when they finally sat drinking their coffee, and Kerry chose this moment to leap in with the question which had been troubling her for most of her life.

'Why did you walk out on us?'

Her father looked up from his coffee and frowned. 'Is that what your mother told you?'

'She never mentioned the subject unless I asked, and all she said was that you'd left and gone to Australia.'

'I never walked out on you and your mother, Kerry.' He shook his greying head and smiled twistedly, then he corrected himself. 'Well, in a way, I suppose, I did walk out on you, but there was a lot more to it than that.'

'I'd like to know what happened,' she said, putting down her cup and observing him closely when he started to speak.

'The company I was working for at that time offered me a five-year contract in Australia. It was a chance of a lifetime and I couldn't turn it down. I could take my family with me—that was part of the deal, but your mother had just been offered a partnership in the law firm she worked for, and she felt it would harm her career at that point if she left.'

'So you left without us,' Kerry filled in for him when he lapsed into a thoughtful silence.

'Yes, I left without you and your mother,' he confirmed grimly. 'After a month I wrote to her and begged her to join me, but she refused. I wrote to her again. I said that if she loved me she'd join me, and she wrote back saying that if I loved her I'd never have left in the first place. There was an element of stubbornness on both sides, I guess, but during that first year in Australia we'd said so many hurtful things to each other in our letters that, in the end, we agreed that we needed the five years away from each other to decide finally whether our marriage was worth saving.'

'Who made the decision to end it?' asked Kerry.

'I did,' he confessed, the grimness deepening about his mouth. 'Your mother had said that when the job in Australia was finished I could come back if I wanted to and we'd try to sort things out; but five years is a long time, and I'd become so disillusioned and embittered that there didn't seem to be anything left to sort out. I'd been offered the opportunity to start my own business, and by that time I'd also met the woman I'm married to now, so I decided to cut my ties by writing to your mother and asking her to give me a divorce.'

'And you promptly forgot about me as well,' Kerry added bitterly.

'No, I never forgot you,' he responded with a matching bitterness. 'Your mother won custody of you, and because you hadn't seen me in so many years she and I decided that it would be detrimental to your happiness if you were shunted off periodically to a father you never really knew.'

'I see,' she said, understanding their reasoning all those years ago, but it still hurt.

'Marge, my wife, is a good woman,' he went on. 'She's given me two lovely children, and she's made me very happy, but she could never fill the empty space that your mother left in my life.'

Empty space? Her mother had left an empty space in his life? What was he saying?

'That's another reason why I thought it best that we shouldn't meet,' he explained ruefully. 'I was afraid that Marge would be hurt. You see, Kerry, she's known all these years that I never really stopped loving your mother.'

Kerry felt like weeping. 'Your wife must love you very much,' she said quietly.

'I don't deserve her,' he scowled, moving his shoulders as if his jacket had suddenly become too tight for him.

'I don't think my mother ever really stopped loving you either,' she said, fiddling with the clasp of her evening bag.

'You must be mistaken, Kerry,' he brushed aside her theory with a faintly cynical smile.

'I don't think so.' She opened her bag and saw her father's face pale in the candle-light as he noticed the heart-shaped gold pendant dangling on a chain from her fingers. Engraved on the back of the pendant were the words 'Jan, I love you, Ed' and the date was two years before Kerry's birth. 'Mum always wore this pendant,' she explained with a catch in her voice as she passed it to her father across the table. 'She never went anywhere without it, and she was clutching it in her hand when she died. Do you think she would have attached such importance to it if she hadn't cared?'

'But *why*?' her father groaned, naked pain in his eyes when he read the inscription on the back of the pendant. 'Why did she let me believe she no longer loved me?'

'I don't know.'

If you love something, let it go. Kerry was reminded once more of her mother's words. Was it possible that her mother had set her father free in the hope that he would return to her? 'Perhaps she was afraid to tell you how she felt about you because she thought you'd stopped caring and didn't want to embarrass you. Maybe she hoped that, despite everything, you'd eventually come back and give your marriage a second chance.'

'That sounds like Janet's way of reasoning,' he agreed.

'Would you like to keep the pendant?' she asked him.

He shook his head and handed it back to her. 'You keep it, Kerry. Keep it as a reminder never to let stubborn pride come between you and the one you love.'

That was good advice, but what was she supposed to do when the one she loved would never love her in return?

Despite all their earlier misgivings Kerry and her father had had so much to talk about that she arrived home late that Thursday evening. She'd also had so much to think about that she could not sleep, and she had lain awake for most of the night, but she was at the airport the following day, as she had promised, to see her father off.

'Thank you for coming all this way to talk to me,' she said, her throat tightening when it was time for him to leave.

'I'm glad I came.' Edward Nelson smiled down at his daughter and clasped her hands in his. 'I guess the next time we meet you'll be married to that fellow who barged into my Sydney office and read me my rights.'

Kerry stiffened. 'I'm afraid you've got the wrong impression. Max and I aren't—we're not——'

'If you're going to tell me you're not in love with him, then you're forgetting I saw the look on your face last night when I mentioned his name.'

'It's a one-sided thing.' She hid her pain behind a forced smile. 'Max doesn't love me.'

'Doesn't he?' Edward Nelson looked surprised, but the announcement of his flight ended the conversation there, and he drew Kerry into a quick, unexpected embrace to which she responded with an odd sense of belonging. 'Take care of yourself, baby,' he said.

Baby! The word roused a memory which had been buried too deep for her to recall on her own. Her father had called her baby; never Kerry. Hang on, baby, Daddy's going to give you a piggyback ride to your bed!

She could remember it now with a stinging clarity, and tears misted her eyes as she watched her father walk away from her. He turned once and waved. She waved back. And then he was gone.

Kerry lingered in the airport building until she saw the thirteen thirty-five flight to Sydney, Australia, taxi out on to the runway. People were crowding around noisily in the observation area, waving to friends and family in the Boeing even though they could not be seen, but Kerry stood there like a statue, choking back the tears and wishing back a time which was now gone forever.

'That's so typical of Max,' Kathleen remarked laughingly when Kerry told her about Max contacting her father in Australia. 'My brother's always had an over-zealous sense of justice.'

A sense of justice. Yes, that was all it had been. A touching sense of justice.

Kerry stretched her denim-clad legs out towards the winter sun, which was slanting in through the library windows and crossed her booted feet at the ankles. She sipped her tea, and for the third time that Sunday afternoon she had to drag her glance away from the photograph on the low cupboard between the tall windows in an attempt to concentrate solely on Kathleen Stafford. 'It was kind of Max to go out of his way to help me,' she said, controlling her features with some difficulty.

'I received a telephone call this morning from one of Max's acquaintances in Australia.'

There was something in Kathleen's voice that filled Kerry with a strange uneasiness. What did it mean? Was she imagining it, or had something happened that she ought to know about?

'How is Max?' she asked with a forced casualness.

'He's in hospital.'

Icy fingers curled about Kerry's heart and her mind leapt frantically from one frightening possibility to the next as she drew her feet in and sat up. Her face had paled visibly, and her hands were shaking to the extent that she had to deposit her cup on the low table beside her chair for fear of spilling the remainder of her tea into her lap or, worse still, on to the expensive Persian rug at her feet.

'What's wrong?' she asked with an abruptness born of fear. 'What happened?'

'A horse unseated him two days ago and he's broken his collar-bone.'

Relief washed over Kerry, and she sagged weakly into her chair. During the weeks following her father's visit she had been doing everything possible to come to terms with her fate. She knew she could never have Max, but that did not stop her from thinking about him, neither did it ease the longing that lay like a heavy weight in her breast during the long, dark hours of every night.

Would it ever end?

She looked up and realised to her horror that Kathleen had, for a long time, been studying her speculatively over the rim of her teacup.

'Are you in love with my brother, Kerry?'

Kerry stiffened. That question jolted her almost as much as the terrifying thought that something might have happened to Max.

'Are you?' Kathleen prompted gently when Kerry failed to answer her.

'No! No, of course not! It's ridiculous to even think it!'

'I don't happen to think it's so ridiculous,' Kathleen responded quietly as she leaned forward in her chair to place her empty cup on the tray. 'I think you're in love with Max. In fact, I'm convinced of it.'

Kerry shook her head agitatedly. 'I don't know where you got that crazy idea from, but you're wrong, and——'

'If you're not in love with him,' Kathleen cut in firmly, 'then explain to me why you can't seem to take your eyes off his photograph whenever you're here. And tell me also why you looked like death when I mentioned that he was in hospital.'

Kerry tried to speak, but the words lodged painfully in her throat, and she got up instead to stand at the window. Kathleen's beautiful garden had changed with the seasons from the brilliance of summer through the rich gold of autumn and into the drab green bareness of winter.

More than four months had passed since the last time she had seen Max. She could not get him out of her system, but she was also beginning to have difficulty identifying her feelings.

'Have I been that obvious?' she heard herself saying.

'Not at first, my dear,' Kathleen assured her. 'I admit I've had my suspicions all along, but I wasn't sure until now.'

'Please...' Kerry turned, the rawness of her voice mirrored in her eyes. 'Please don't tell him. I don't want him to know.'

Kathleen studied her pensively for what seemed like an eternity before she said gravely, 'If that's what you want, then you have my word that he shan't hear it from me.'

'I actually don't know how I feel any more,' Kerry confessed as she returned to her chair and sat down heavily. 'It's been such a long time, and lately there's so much anger in me that I'm beginning to wonder if what I'm experiencing isn't just a childish hankering for something I know I can't have.'

'I can't speak for Max since he hasn't confided in me,' Kathleen said while she poured them a fresh cup of tea. 'I know he's always considered it unfair to marry a woman and then expect her to put up with his nomadic way of life, but, in a way, I think he does care for you. Why else would he have asked me to stay in touch with you?' Kathleen put down the teapot and raised her fingers to her lips, her eyes widening with alarm. 'Oh, dear! I shouldn't have said that!'

Kerry gripped the wooden arms of her chair when she felt that now familiar explosion of anger inside her. 'Max asked you to keep tabs on me and report back to him? Is that it? And is that the sole reason for our friendship?'

'Oh, no! No, it isn't like that at all!' Kathleen protested anxiously. 'If I didn't enjoy your company I could have stayed in touch in many other ways which wouldn't have necessitated having to meet with you, or invite you to my home. As for keeping tabs on you and reporting back to Max... well, that—that's simply dreadful!'

'But you've discussed me when he's phoned.'

'He would ask me if I've seen you or heard from you, and I might tell him you came to tea or that we met in town for lunch. That was all he would ask, and that was all I ever told him.' Kathleen's hand shook slightly as she handed Kerry her tea. 'Max has known many other women, Kerry, but he's never made an effort to stay in touch with any of them, and that's why I'm so certain that he must care for you.'

'Don't make me hope again, Kathleen. The only thing Max really cares about is his freedom, and I don't intend to forget that.'

The late afternoon shadows had lengthened across the lawn, and there was a biting coldness in the air that made Kerry shiver beneath her blue woollen sweater when she left the house and walked out to where she had parked her station-wagon.

'Don't let your feelings for my wayward brother mar our friendship,' Kathleen said when Kerry unlocked the door to the Peugeot, then she leaned forward unexpectedly and kissed Kerry on her cool cheek. 'Regardless of what you may believe, I've grown very fond of you, Kerry, and I wish there was something I could do to make my brother realise what a perfect wife you'd be.'

It was on a bitterly cold Saturday night towards the end of July when Kerry dried herself after her bath and pulled on her long winter nightdress. She had completed all her assignments, and she was seriously thinking of taking Josie's advice. She needed a long holiday in warm, tranquil surroundings where she could sort out the tangled mess her life had become.

She crawled wearily into bed and slid down beneath the duvet with a sigh on her lips. She was so tired, so very tired of trying to find forgetfulness in the long hours she worked, and so tired living a life with no purpose in mind.

She might as well be dead.

The shrill ringing of the telephone sliced through her disconsolate thoughts, and she sat up with a start to glance at the small bedside clock. Eleven-fifteen! No one ever called her at this time of the night!

Her heart was pounding and the persistent ringing of the telephone jarred her nerves as the leapt out of bed to run barefooted from her room. She snapped on the light in the hall, and almost knocked over a vase of chrysanthemums in her haste to snatch up the receiver.

'Kerry Nelson speaking,' she said into the mouthpiece, wondering if she sounded as wary as she felt.

'Hello, Kerry.'

That voice!

Her knees buckled beneath her weight, and she slid down along the cold, plastered wall to sit in a crumpled heap on the carpeted floor.

CHAPTER TEN

'HELLO? Kerry? *Damn*! These telephones are all the same!' There was frustration and anger in Max's voice amid a discordant thumping as if his fist had connected several times with the public telephone's metal casing. 'Can you hear me, Kerry? Hello? Are you there?'

Kerry heard it all as if from a distance while she fought her way up through that blanket of darkness which had threatened to envelop her. 'I'm here.' Her lips moved, but no sound emerged and, clearing her throat, she tried again. 'I'm here, Max.'

'What? I can't hear you!'

'I said, I'm here,' she managed in a louder voice.

'Thank God!' he groaned. 'After three unsuccessful attempts to get through to you I was beginning to think I had another dud telephone.'

Kerry placed her hand over her thudding heart, willing it to be still. 'Where are you calling from?'

'My plane got in about fifteen minutes ago, and I'm still here at Jan Smuts airport.'

'I didn't think you'd be arriving back so soon. You said you——'

'I must see you tonight, Kerry,' he cut across her inane chatter. 'I've got to talk to you. It's important.'

Another assignment? What else! Kerry felt like weeping, but the tears that stung her eyelids had their origin in the storm of anger that was beginning to sweep through her until her insides shook.

'If you're thinking of offering me an assignment, then the answer is no, and as for seeing you at this hour of the night the answer is also no!'

She slammed down the receiver, and a dry, choking sob passed her lips as she lowered her forehead on to her raised knees.

She sat like that for a few seconds, hugging her legs against her body and rocking herself, then she manoeuvred herself into a kneeling position and reached in under the small table to disconnect the telephone. It started ringing again, but it rang just once before Kerry tugged at the wall connection, and then it was silent.

Her body was racked with tremors when she got back into bed again and drew the duvet up to beneath her chin, but she could not stop shaking.

How *dared* he? How dared Max walk out of her life and then believe he could calmly walk back into it again five months later? No! She was not going to let him do this to her! She was not going to let the torment start all over again!

Kerry could not sleep. The bare branches of the jacaranda tree outside her window were stirring in the breeze, casting a moving shadow across her ceiling, and she lay awake, staring at those sometimes grotesque, groping fingers in the moonlight. She knew somehow that this night was not going to end with that telephone call from Max. She knew it, and she dreaded it.

She lay rigid beneath the duvet, her ears straining to catch any unfamiliar sound in and around the house, and the tension inside her escalated alarmingly when she eventually heard a car stop at her gate a few minutes before midnight.

The engine was left running, the drone of the powerful motor disturbing the silence as much as the sound of a car door being opened and slammed shut moments later, and then the car was being driven off again.

Were those Max's familiar footsteps on the paved courtyard approaching her front door, or was she listening to the sound of her own heart drumming in her ears?

The loose tile on the shallow step snapped its usual warning, and Kerry curled herself into an anxious ball beneath the duvet, her hands pressed firmly over her ears. The doorbell chimed. The sound was muffled, but it still succeeded in jolting her as if several volts of electricity had suddenly charged through her body.

Kerry slid lower beneath the duvet as she heard the doorbell chime again and again. After a minute or two the chime was replaced by a persistent hammering which she felt certain was loud enough to awaken her neighbours.

God, what am I supposed to do? she thought desperately.

Never let stubborn pride come between you and the one you love. That was what her father had said, but this had nothing to do with stubborn pride. This was an act of self-preservation!

Coward! her conscience chided her while the hammering on her door persisted at regular intervals. *Coward*?

Kerry flung back the duvet and snapped on the bedside light before she pushed her feet into her soft mules. 'I'm not a coward!' she muttered fiercely to herself as she pulled on her loose-fitting robe and zipped it up the front.

The hammering on the front door desisted the instant she switched on the light in the hall. She was angry now. Anger was her only weapon against that frightened fluttering in her breast, and anger was the only effective suppressant for those forbidden emotions.

'Who is it?' she demanded sharply.

'You know damn well who it is!' There was a harsh but controlled fury in that familiar male voice on the other side of the door. 'It's Max, so open up!'

'Go away!' she instructed on a shrill note of panic. 'I told you I didn't want to see you!'

'If you don't open this door, Kerry,' he growled his warning, 'I'll cause a commotion loud enough for the entire neighbourhood to hear.'

That was not an idle threat—she could hear it in the tone of his voice, and she leaned forward despairingly to press her hot forehead against the cool wooden door. She was shaking, but it was not because of the cold, and her palms felt clammy as she placed them flat against the door in an unconsciously defensive gesture.

'Kerry! Don't say I didn't warn you!'

She heard the sole of his shoe scraping across the ceramic tiles on her small patio. What was he going to do? Kick the door in?

'All *right*! Wait! I'm opening the door!' Kerry shouted back, nervous haste making her fumble with the lock.

She had barely snapped back the safety catch when the door was pushed open from the outside. Max, suitcase in hand, was suddenly dwarfing her small entrance hall. He was wearing a thick grey overcoat with the collar turned up at his throat, and there was a dark fury—and something else she could not define—in the eyes that raked her from head to foot.

Kerry felt hot and cold simultaneously, and she backed away against the wall for support while she feasted hungrily on those ruggedly handsome features which had haunted her days and her nights for so many months.

Her body was sending out signals—signals of a need so long suppressed, and she was suddenly afraid for herself as she stood there staring up at the wide-shouldered man who was towering over her.

'Close the door,' she snapped, shivering in the icy draught of night air that nipped at her nose and slid its chilly fingers up underneath her full-length gown. 'You're letting in the cold.'

Max deposited his suitcase on the carpeted floor before he closed the door to shut out the cold, and Kerry's sensitive nerves jarred at the sound of the safety catch snapping into position.

'You hung up on me,' he accused darkly.

'Well, what did you expect me to do when you call me out of the blue at this time of night?' she stormed back at him. 'And if it's a photographer you need then you'd better look elsewhere, because I'm not available.'

'I didn't say I needed a photographer.'

'You implied it.'

'No, I didn't,' he corrected her with mockery in his heavy-lidded eyes. 'You assumed it.'

'All right, so I assumed it!' She could feel her heart thumping into the cold wall against her back. 'Why else would you have called me?'

'We'll talk about that later,' he said, taking off his overcoat and draping it over his suitcase. His brown suede jacket and corduroy trousers fitted him perfectly, but he looked as if he had lost weight. 'Let me just look at you, Kerry.'

Her hair had tumbled in a silvery, untidy mass about her shoulders, and she felt awkward suddenly about her state of undress, but Max seemed more interested in those shadowy hollows beneath her eyes and that unaccustomed tightness about her usually soft mouth.

His dark, probing glance finally shifted lower to where those small, firm mounds were jutting against the brushed nylon of her robe, and she was dismayed to feel her breasts swelling beneath his gaze, the nipples hardening with the desire to know his touch again. Memories flooded her mind, unleashing a heated sensation inside her that spiralled into her loins, and her breath locked in her throat as Max's glance dipped lower.

A weakness invaded her limbs, and she knew that if she did not do something quickly she would make a complete fool of herself.

'Now that you've seen me I suggest you say what you have to say, and go!' Did that cold, savagely controlled voice belong to her?

Max seemed to flinch as if she had slapped him, then a speculative look entered his eyes. 'You're angry.'

'You're damn right I'm angry!'

'Why?'

That question floored Kerry completely. To answer it she would have to lay her soul bare, and that was the last thing she wanted to do at this moment.

Her anger drained away slowly, leaving her vulnerable without its protection, and her shoulders sagged defeatedly. 'It's late, Max, and I'm tired, so let's not drag this out for longer than we absolutely have to.'

'Would you make me a cup of coffee?'

A refusal sprang to her lips, but compassion silenced her as her mind registered certain facts which it had ignored before.

Max's eyes were sunk in his head, and the hollows beneath his cheekbones seemed to deepen the grooves running from his aquiline nose down to his firmly chiselled mouth. He looked exhausted, as if he had neither slept nor eaten for days, and Kerry suddenly felt ashamed of herself for wanting to deny him a cup of coffee.

'Come through to the kitchen,' she invited, turning her back on his disturbing appearance to lead the way.

'I haven't had a bath or a change of clothing in two days, and I'm beginning to feel a bit gritty after the long flight,' he said when she switched on the kitchen light. 'Do you think I could have a bath and change my clothes while you're making the coffee?'

He had a nerve! He had a fabulous apartment in the city, but instead he was invading her meagre lodgings in the middle of the night, requesting a cup of coffee and the use of her bathroom. This really was too, *too* much!

'Just make yourself at home,' she replied caustically, unplugging the electric kettle and running water into it. 'The bathroom leads off my bedroom. It's the door on your left down the passage, and you'll find a supply of clean towels in the bathroom cupboard.'

Max collected his suitcase in the hall, and then his slow, heavy footsteps disappeared down the passage to Kerry's bedroom. She heard him running water above the hiss of the electric kettle, and she delayed making the instant coffee until much later when she heard the familiar gurgle of water draining out of the bath.

She glanced at the digital clock on the eye-level oven. Twelve-thirty. Dear God, she was so tired, and yet she felt so... so *alive*!

Stop it, Kerry! she told herself. He's here for a purpose that has nothing to do with making you feel alive again, or wanted, or loved. Don't get your hopes up, my girl, because Maxwell Harper has no intention of inviting you into his busy, nomadic life on a permanent basis.

Kerry made the coffee and waited. Silence. It made her curious, and she left the kitchen to walk quickly and silently down the passage to her room.

'Max?' She called his name softly, but when there was no reply she went inside.

He was lying on his back, sprawled across her double bed in clean blue denims, a grey woollen sweater, and with no shoes on his feet. His eyes were closed, his dark, heavy lashes deepening the shadows above his cheekbones, and from the slow, shallow rise and fall of his chest she could tell he was fast asleep.

What nerve! she thought, wanting to laugh, but instead her throat constricted and her eyes filled with tears.

'Oh, Max!' she whispered his name unsteadily, sliding the duvet out from under his feet and covering him up before she switched off the bedside light.

She fetched a couple of blankets and pillows out of the passage cupboard, and made up a bed for herself on the sofa in the lounge, but she lay awake for a long time, listening to those familiar sounds in and around the house. It felt so good to know that Max was under the same roof as her that she was curiously at peace with herself for the first time in months.

Don't get any ideas, Kerry, she remonstrated with herself. It's only for tonight. Tomorrow he'll be gone again, and then you're going to be right back where you started.

It was a disquieting thought, and she brushed it aside mentally. It was enough to know that Max was in the same house with her, even if it was only for one night, and she went to sleep on that thought.

She awakened at six on the Sunday morning. It was still dark outside, and she felt a little confused at finding herself on the sofa, but then she remembered.

Max! Max was sleeping in her bed!

She got up quickly, folded the blankets and put them away with the pillows in the passage cupboard before she went through to the kitchen. She switched on the light and stared for a moment at the two untouched mugs of coffee on her kitchen table. One of them had grown a dusky brown skin overnight, and she pulled a face as she emptied the cups into the sink and switched on the electric kettle to make herself a fresh cup of coffee.

Max was still asleep when she entered her bedroom, and her heart contracted painfully at the sight of him. He was lying in virtually the same position she had left him in the night before, and she stepped quietly over his open suitcase on the floor to take an old navy tracksuit and canvas shoes out of her cupboard.

She washed and changed in the bathroom, and Max was beginning to stir when she returned to the kitchen to start breakfast.

It was seven-thirty when Kerry turned from the stove to see Max wandering barefooted into the kitchen. He was still wearing the denims and grey knitted sweater he had slept in, his hair lay untidily across his broad forehead, and there was a sheepish grin on his face as he seated himself at the table which she had laid earlier.

'I'm afraid I commandeered your bed last night,' he apologised.

'So I noticed,' she said drily, intensely aware of those dark eyes following her when she switched on the electric kettle to bring the water to the boil again.

'I was so tired after I'd bathed and changed that I thought I'd lie down for a second or two, but I must have fallen asleep immediately. I'm sorry.'

'Coffee?' she asked, ignoring his apology.

'Thank you.'

She spooned instant coffee into a mug, added boiling water, and placed the mug of black, sugarless coffee on the table in front of Max. His glance drew hers and held it for a second before she looked away, but her nerves were flaring in response to the warmth she had seen in his eyes.

Don't let him do this to you! Kerry warned herself when she turned back to the stove. Don't let him soften you up only to walk away from you again!

'That smells good,' he said after a long, awkward silence had elapsed. 'What is it?'

'Cheese omelette.' She placed a rack of toast on the table, and used her oven gloves to remove the heated plates from the warming drawer below the oven. She was scooping the omelettes into their plates when she noticed that Max was flexing his right shoulder tentatively, and concern drove everything else temporarily from her mind. 'Is your shoulder still causing you a lot of discomfort?' she asked him.

'It's healed nicely, but it tends to stiffen up during the night.' Max's smile was faintly amused when Kerry joined him at the table. 'I suppose Kathleen told you?'

'Yes,' she said, her face a rigid, polite mask when she passed him the toast and the butter. 'Does Kathleen know you're back?'

'No, she doesn't.'

Kerry found that odd. He had stayed in touch with his sister during these months he had been away, keeping her up to date with his movements. Why had he not given her the date of his return?

The questions churning through her mind were becoming too numerous to cope with, and she put down her knife and fork to meet Max's steady glance across the table. 'What was so important last night that you felt it couldn't wait for this morning?' she asked.

'I think we should eat first and talk later,' he said, biting into his toast with those strong white teeth, and chewing it a few times before he swallowed it down.

'If you're trying to trap me into accepting another assignment, then you might as well forget it, because I——'

'As a matter of fact, I do have another assignment for you.'

Kerry's anger rose sharply at Max's calm interjection, and she made no attempt to disguise it. 'The answer is no, Max, and this time there's no way you can blackmail me into it again.'

'This is quite delicious,' he said, unperturbed by her remark as he speared a piece of his omelette and popped it into his mouth.

'I think you must be one of the most infuriating men I've ever known!' she snapped.

'I think you're incredibly beautiful when you're angry, and it certainly makes you all the more desirable.' His eyes left hers to rest on the agitated rise and fall of her breasts beneath her tracksuit-top, and the sensuous smile curving his mouth made her nipples harden in response.

'Damn you, Max!' she exploded in a furious hiss, her hands clenching on the table beside her plate and her eyes a flint-like blue. '*Damn* you for storming back into my life just when it was beginning to settle back to some sort of normality!'

'Is there such a thing as normality?' he demanded, hollow-faced and grim. 'God knows, I had it once in my life, but I can't seem to find it now.'

What was he saying? How was she supposed to interpret that statement? Kerry's anger subsided a fraction while her bewildered mind was trying to grasp at something that remained tantalisingly beyond its reach.

'I think we'd better eat our breakfast,' she said, picking up her knife and fork with hands that were not quite steady. 'I have a tendency to get things confused on an empty stomach.'

His taut features relaxed slightly. 'Maybe I should take advantage of that confusion to state my case.'

'Don't try it!' she warned, her eyes flashing blue fire at him, and he put down his knife and fork to raise his hands in a defensive gesture.

'Relax, Kerry,' he laughed shortly. 'It was merely a thought.'

They finished their breakfast in silence, but Kerry was aware of Max's brooding glances resting on her from time to time. It made her feel intensely nervous and uneasy, and they were drinking their coffee when she looked up again to find those darkly mysterious eyes observing her.

'My father was here on a brief visit a month ago.' She said the first thing that came to mind.

'I'm glad.'

'He said I had you to thank for bringing him to his senses.'

'I saw how much his rejection had hurt you, and he needed no more than a gentle shove to steer them in the right direction,' he shrugged.

A gentle shove? According to her father there had been nothing gentle about it.

'Thank you, Max. I doubt if you'll ever know how much I appreciate what you did for me.' She looked into those brown eyes flecked with gold. What was he thinking? What lay behind those brooding eyes, and how was it going to affect her? The tension of not knowing was becoming too much to bear. 'Why are you looking at me like that?'

'I have an assignment for you, Kerry.'

Her body stiffened, everything inside her rejecting his statement. 'I told you, I'm not interested.'

'It's a permanent assignment.'

'I refuse to accept this assignment, permanent or otherwise, even if it's——'

'I want you to marry me.'

'—the last assignment I'm ever . . .' She stared at him, her eyes widening as his calmly spoken words skimmed the surface of her stunned, incredulous mind, and she was glad she was seated when she felt the kitchen sway precariously beneath her. 'What did you say?' she demanded weakly.

'Marry me, Kerry.'

Something was dreadfully wrong. This could not be Maxwell Harper talking; this was her tormented mind playing cruel tricks on her. 'Are *you* crazy, or am *I*?' she gasped.

'I'd rather be crazy *with* you than continue to go crazy *without* you,' he replied, and Kerry shook her head in disbelief.

'I—I don't believe this.'

'Believe it!' He reached across the table to capture her hands in his. 'You asked me once if I ever felt lonely. Do you remember?'

'I remember it very well.' She freed her hands from the warm, disturbing clasp of his fingers and rose unsteadily from her chair to look out of the kitchen window. She was staring at the bare stems of the grapevine that snaked up along the garden wall, but she was seeing again that look of derision on Max's face that night in the dining-room of the Maltahöhe Hotel. 'You said that loneliness is a state of mind that lends itself to inactivity.'

'I was wrong, Kerry.' The legs of his chair scraped across the tiled floor and she turned warily to see him step around the table to lessen the distance between them. 'I've worked my butt off these past months, and I was seldom alone, but I found I was lonely because you weren't there to share it all with me.'

'Don't... do this... to me, Max.' Her heart had recognised the truth in his eyes and in his voice, and her body was beginning to respond to it, but her cautious mind remained sceptical. 'You expect me to believe you, but you never once tried to get in touch with me during these past five months.'

'I didn't want to get in touch with you because I was determined to forget you, but for some obscure reason I asked my sister to stay in contact with you.' His eyes were pin-points of fire, searing her body through the tracksuit material and touching hidden nerves before returning hungrily to her face. 'To be brutally honest with you, Kerry, there've been many women in my life, but my interest always waned long before we parted company. With you it was different. I was reluctant to leave you in Windhoek and, no matter how much I tried, I just couldn't forget you. You were with me wherever I went and in everything I did. You even haunted my dreams until I believed I'd go mad thinking about you... *wanting* you.'

The atmosphere in Kerry's small kitchen was charged with emotion. Max reached out to her, but she shrank back against the low cupboard. 'Don't touch me!' she warned in a strangled voice.

His hands settled on the cupboard, trapping her between his arms without touching her, but every tiny nerve in her body was suddenly quivering in response to his nearness.

'Last night it was enough just to be under the same roof with you and to smell the scent of you where you'd lain on the bed, but this morning I have a desperate need to hold you and to feel the soft warmth of your skin beneath my hands.' The deep velvet of his voice was seductive. It assaulted her senses and threatened to dull her mind. 'I want to hold you and kiss you all over. I want to feel you tremble when I lie with you, and then I want to lose myself in you.'

'*No!*' she cried out, rejecting the intimacy he was suggesting, but her body had already betrayed her. Her body craved that intimacy; it was hot and throbbing with a need so intense that she clenched her hands at her sides in a physical attempt to control her rampant emotions.

'I'm not blind, my darling,' Max murmured, his breath cool against her damp forehead. 'Your lips may say no to me, but your body has been saying yes ever since I walked into the kitchen this morning. Admit it, my love.'

My *darling*? My *love*? He had said those words with such tenderness that her flagging resistance collapsed like a house of cards caught in a breeze. She loved him—she no longer had any doubt in her mind about that, and she wanted him. And, for the moment, that was enough.

'You're wrong,' she contradicted him in a voice she could not raise above a whisper. 'My body's been saying yes since last night.'

Max drew a rasping breath, his eyes darkening, and then she was in his arms, her mouth seeking his just as his sought hers. Her hips moved involuntarily against his aroused body, conveying the extent of her need, and he groaned with the urgency of his own desire as he lifted her in his arms and carried her from the kitchen to her bedroom.

They undressed hurriedly and in between fevered kisses, flinging their clothes to the floor in their desperate haste to feel flesh against flesh and, when they fell across the bed, their bodies melded with a readiness which the long months of separation had heightened to an explosive pitch.

Their release came too soon to satisfy that hunger inside them, and they made love again, but this time the pace was slow as they savoured each caress as if it were the last.

Max did everything he had promised, and more. He kissed her all over, until not an inch of her body had been left unexplored. His teeth nipped at her heated, responsive flesh, heightening her excitement, and then he kissed her intimately.

Kerry's gasp of surprise ended in a strangled moan as the most exquisite sensations cascaded through her, but she felt no embarrassment. This was Max. This was the man she loved with every part of her being, and what he was doing seemed so right that nothing would make her believe it could be wrong.

'Max!' she cried out his name, her breathing shallow and erratic, and her hands clutching at his broad shoulders when she felt her desire for him slipping beyond her control. 'Oh, Max! Please! Take me now!'

'Not yet, my darling,' he murmured throatily, shifting over her and taking possession of her mouth to heighten her excitement with the thrust and parry of his tongue.

Kerry moaned into his mouth, and her body writhed beneath his as her desire reached a near-intolerable peak.

'Damn you, Max!' she gasped when he eased his mouth from hers. 'Don't torment me like this!'

He smiled, his dark eyes glazed with desire, then he entered her with a slowness which in itself was a torment. 'I love you, Kerry,' he said convincingly.

Joy and desire was an odd mixture, but her flushed cheeks were wet with tears when Max's thrusting body brought them both to a shattering climax.

When their laboured breathing subsided he lifted his head to look at her. 'You've been crying,' he observed with concern, kissing away the tears which were still hovering on her lashes.

'I didn't think I could ever be this happy,' she confessed.

'Neither did I,' he sighed, covering their damp bodies with the duvet.

Kerry felt content to lie in his arms and to savour the warmth of his body against her own, but her contentment finally gave way to those questions which were nagging to be answered.

She eased herself away from him and sat propped up against the pillows with the duvet drawn up to beneath her chin. 'Did you complete the television programme you were filming in Australia?' she asked.

'No, I didn't.' Max frowned as if he disliked the feeling that his arms were empty. 'Five months in Australia without you was about as much as I could take.'

'So you'll have to go back.'

'It can wait.' His glance met hers and she saw the question in his eyes before he voiced it. 'Will you marry me, Kerry?'

She wanted to say yes, but there was something she needed to know before she could give him her answer.

'I love you, Max. No, wait!' She held him off with a hand against his solid, hair-roughened chest when he would have pulled her down into his arms again. 'I love you enough not to want to tie you down to something you don't really want.'

'Are you suggesting that we simply live together?'

'No, of course not, but...' She swallowed long and hard at that aching restriction in her throat. 'You told me once that marriage wouldn't blend well with your profession.'

There was remembered torment in the eyes that held hers as he took her hand in his and traced the fine white scar across her palm with the tip of his tongue. 'I didn't know then how empty life would be without you there to give meaning to it, and I've had five long months to realise that no problem is insurmountable when you love someone as much as I love you. Besides...' he smiled suddenly, and there was a devilish gleam in his eyes '...marriage to you means that I'll never again have to hire another photographer.'

'What if we should have children?' she asked, ignoring his remark. 'I don't know about you, Max, but I know I would eventually want children, and you said you wouldn't like the idea of not being there for your children if they should need you.'

'There are such things as nannies and tutors, and just think what an education it would be for our children to travel the world with us.'

His devilish smile was becoming infectious, and her lips quirked in response. 'It seems to me you've thought of everything.'

'I've had a long time to think,' he said, raising himself up on to one elbow as he slipped his hand beneath the duvet to trail his fingers along her shapely thigh and up across her flat stomach to cup her breast in his palm. 'My thoughts of you were all I had, but having you in the flesh is a million times better.'

'Oh, Max,' she sighed, her heart in her eyes as she combed her fingers lovingly through the greying hair at his temples. 'I missed you so much.'

His fingers tightened in a gentle warning against her breast. 'I'm still waiting for an answer to my proposal.'

'These past months have been hell without you, Max. I haven't been alive, I've merely existed, and I can't think of anything I want more than to marry you and spend the rest of my life with you,' she confessed, loving the feel of his thumb raking across her hardened nipple. 'I think I knew the first time we met that I'd eventually feel this way about you, and it scared me to think that I might become so dependent on someone else for my very existence.'

He released her suddenly, and there was a certain arrogance in the way he lay back against the pillows with his hands locked behind his head. 'I have an assignment for you, Kerry Ann Nelson,' he told her.

'Do you, Maxwell Jonathan Harper?' she responded in a similar vein.

'I'm thinking of spending three weeks in Mauritius before returning to Australia.' His eyebrows arched mockingly. 'Want to tag along and make it a honeymoon?'

'Just you try and stop me!' she warned, laughter in her eyes as she moved towards him, and he caught her in his arms, lifting her on top of him so that she lay with her legs between his and his heated arousal against that part of her body which was becoming equally aroused.

She lowered her mouth to his, her lips parting, and their tongues engaged in an erotic play which sharpened their senses once again to the needs of their bodies.

Max groaned deep down in his throat when she moved her hips against him, and he slid his hands down under the duvet to stay the action. 'What you're doing is sweet heaven, Kerry,' he murmured throatily against her mouth. 'You'd better marry me as soon as I can arrange it.'

A sobering thought entered Kerry's mind. Marriage was the ultimate commitment, and she could not enter into it with a lie on her conscience.

'There's something I have to tell you, Max,' she said, lifting her head to look at him, but a ridiculous shyness took possession of her and she could not meet his eyes. 'That night in Usakos. I—I'd never slept with a man before.'

His chest heaved beneath her. 'So I didn't imagine it after all.'

She looked at him now, her eyes anxious. 'Don't be angry, Max—please! I loved you and I wanted you so much. Nothing else mattered in the end.'

He brushed that veil of silky fair hair away from her face with gentle fingers. 'My sweetest, dearest Kerry,' he murmured softly, his smile so tender that it touched her soul as nothing had ever done before. 'I adore you, and I'm glad I was the first.'

The palm trees on the Mauritian beach stood etched in a stark silhouette against the fiery hue of the setting sun, and Kerry sighed with the beauty of it as she leaned back in the circle of her husband's strong arms.

Their honeymoon was almost over. They had spent three idyllic weeks in Mauritius, and soon they would have to leave.

Kerry tilted her head to one side to look up into Max's face. His eyes were on the far horizon as if he could not wait to see what lay beyond it, but Kerry was not disturbed by that look. She knew that Max would be taking her with him, because they belonged together, and there was peace and contentment in that knowledge.